William Howard Russell

The Adventures of Doctor Brady

Vol. I

William Howard Russell

The Adventures of Doctor Brady
Vol. I

ISBN/EAN: 9783743420090

Manufactured in Europe, USA, Canada, Australia, Japa

Cover: Foto ©Andreas Hilbeck / pixelio.de

Manufactured and distributed by brebook publishing software (www.brebook.com)

William Howard Russell

The Adventures of Doctor Brady

THE ADVENTURES

OF

DOCTOR BRADY.

BY

WILLIAM HOWARD RUSSELL,

AUTHOR OF

"LETTERS FROM THE CRIMEA," "MY DIARY IN INDIA,"
"MY DIARY NORTH AND SOUTH," ETC. ETC.

IN THREE VOLUMES.

VOL. I.

REPRINTED FROM TINSLEYS' MAGAZINE.

LONDON:
TINSLEY BROTHERS, 18, CATHERINE STREET, STRAND.
1868.

LONDON :
SAVILL, EDWARDS AND CO., PRINTERS, CHANDOS STREET,
COVENT GARDEN.

TO

GENERAL SIR DE LACY EVANS

𝔗𝔥𝔢𝔰𝔢 𝔙𝔬𝔩𝔲𝔪𝔢𝔰 𝔞𝔯𝔢 𝔇𝔢𝔡𝔦𝔠𝔞𝔱𝔢𝔡,

IN MEMORY OF A VALUED FRIENDSHIP,

BY

THE AUTHOR.

LONDON, *March*, 1868.

CONTENTS

OF

THE FIRST VOLUME.

THE ADVENTURES

OF

DOCTOR BRADY.

CHAPTER I.

" MYSELF."

THEY speak of " the mist of years." Is it not
rather a dense dark cloud, through the ever-closing
chinks in which one seeks in vain to discern clearly
all the outlines of the scenery he has left behind him,
and to follow the exact course of the path which
has been trodden once and is never to be retraced?
To my eyes, at least, as I look back there seems a
thick veil up-reared, through rifts in which I can
obtain but glimpses of the past. I am still at that
time of life which men of middle age term its
prime, but I attempt unavailingly to recall the
shapes and forms which once filled the whole expanse of my little world. The recollections of our

childhood are like those we retain of last night's sunset. We remember the beauty which floated in the air in all its golden glories—the rapt delight with which we gazed on the subtle play of light tinted with the hues of heaven, but we cannot summon each element to take its original order in the mutations and progress of the glowing pageant. We can only think of the general impression produced, or dwell on some particular combination perhaps, which lasted for a moment, just as a ruined castle, a clump of trees in a landscape, or an incident in a day's travel are fixed in the mind when all beside that pleased us is forgotten.

My most ancient memory is of a tender, large-eyed face, for which I had a passion when I was about four years old. I remember well the grey eyes, the low, broad brow with bands of black hair surmounted by a white cap, as the Alpine pine-belt is crowned by snowfields—a face, whose expression hour after hour was the source of infinite joy or distress to me; but I cannot remember much more of Honour Flynn, my nurse, than that she was strong of hand and fleet of foot, and that some years later I struggled with exceeding vehemence and wrath to disentangle myself from the embrace of a woman with a freckled face, who caressed me, while great tears rolled down her nose, exclaiming—

"Masther Terry, shure it's your own Honour! your own dear nurse, Honour, darlin', that you used to love so."

Alas! that love had all died out; four years had made a clean sweep of my young affection, and I was almost angry with myself for ever having allowed such a coarse person to have been on intimate terms with me. I can remember, too, a little lake, surrounded by trees, set in the midst of a great meadow, beyond which I can see "our house;" and between me and the lake a swift rivulet, filled with watercresses and sticklebacks, which rippled away over a tiny bar of sand into the larger stream that flowed into the lake. There is a white-headed old man, in a grey coat, with its tails in the water, standing out, as it appears to me, in dreadful depths, waving over his head a whip-like wand of vast proportions, from which flies out in long curves a thin line, flashing on the surface of the stream. There is a spluttering and a plunging after a time at the end of the line, and Macarthy retreats to the bank.

"There, Masther Terry; there's a purty throut for ye! Whist till I get the hook out ov him, that he mightn't hurt ye wid the teeth ov him. Put yer purty little finger in his gill. There! why he's as long as yerself, a'most! Maybe ye'd like to take him up, and show him to the quality, alannah? He's a bewtiful two pounds, that he is. Ould Dan is able to put the comether on them still."

I see that monster of the deep yet: his speckled sides glistening with orange, red, and brown; his awful rows of teeth, his curving snout, his goggle eyes, and velvety dark red gills; and I remember, too, the roar of terror I gave, and the precipitate flight I made through the meadow from the spot where, with a sudden wriggle—recovering a moment's breath ere he died—he flopped his wet tail against my legs, and wallopped in the long grass. I can remember, also, the face of an auburn-haired boy, striving to dash away the firm hand which sought to give an extra polish to its shining skin, reflected in the little mirror in my tiny bed-room, and the secret marches I used to make to gaze on the same portrait, wondering if it ever would be like Dan Macarthy, or old Dr. Noble, whom I had heard once informing the company after dinner that he was the image of me when he was of the same age. I have a photograph taken for my daughter, which tells me that I have since become alarmingly like Dr. Noble, whom at that time I regarded as the greatest sayer of the thing which was not, recorded in any of the story books I had made acquaintance with. It was, I confess, a very great comfort in those days to me to think that by no possibility could I ever become so ridiculously old as Dan Macarthy or Dr. Noble, and from time to time I confirmed any doubts I might have had on the subject by consulting the glass again, flying furtively away when a footstep approached, as if I had an innate consciousness that it was a sin and a shame to look at oneself, as Honour assured me it was. But I was full of sin and shame; my youthful life was stained with them; and conscience frowned at many undetected crimes, in regard to cream and sugar, which never came to light. If I were to set out to catch all the fleeting memories which are passing now, as the shadows of clouds glide over the fields, you would scarce care to join me in the chase. Let me come to the days when life itself began to write its records in those early characters which survive later-formed alphabets. The stems of the long grass seem still to twine round my feet as I think of an early morning walk with a ruddy-faced hale old man and the dainty little maiden on which occasion one of my great offences was detected and punished.

It was a morning so bright and joyous that the exuberance of the blessing causes a fuller beating of the heart and an indefinable sense of happiness and gratitude! Little Mary Butler had been sent over from "the Castle" to stay with us till the "new governess" came. The governesses came and went very often at that time, when little Mary was young and wayward, and Sir Richard was at home.

Mary, kindest and most winning of infant women, had kept her promise, made over our morning meal of "stirabout and milk," and had asked grandfather to let us go and see him fish in the Carra.

"It's that terrible young serpent, Terry, who has put you up to it, Mary. Besides, you'll get your feet wet."

"No, *indeed—indeed*, Doctor, I'll give you my honour," she exclaimed, putting her hand on a puckered plait of white muslin, "I wont; and I wont let Terry fall into the river."

"Oh! in that case, if you give me your honour," quoth my grandfather, gravely, "tell Dan to get the rod. I really will take you

both down to the Carra and kill a trout for
you."

"Kill—I don't like killing," lisped little Mary.
"That was what Cain did to Abel. But I'll look at
you catching them."

"But trout are not Abels, my dear," said grandpapa, smiling. "And besides, they deserve killing
because of all the innocent creatures they kill on
their own account."

The Carra was a forbidden thing. I always longed
to get near it. But the brink was tabooed ever
after I had been forked one day out of a whirling
pool by Dan Macarthy. Many a time since then
had I stolen down to it, crouching in the meadows
to watch the tremendous tenants of its waters in
their splendour, when, detected and pursued, I had
been seized by the still more tremendous Honour,
swift of foot and strong of hand, and the dreadful
words rang in my ear—

"Masther Terry, *this* time I'll shurely tell yer
granddada." But I had seen the stream and listened to its music. I had gazed on the minnows
floating, circling, sailing, darting, and quivering in
the watery crystal, and watched them fly in scurry-
ing fright over the pebbles as the king of all the
sticklebacks, with red gills and breast, and flashing

eyes and bristling spines, made a fierce foray on the covenanting congregation from his lair beneath the bulrush, or a tyrant trout slid from the outer deeps and dashed in a hungry swirl through their ranks.

I was anxious to explain all the wonders of my particular deep to my companion. And so, as the old squire walked along before us, casting his line in vain, for the water was bright and low, and the fish glinted away before him, we two, hand in hand, wandered on and on, Mary picking flowers, and I loitering on purpose and seeking to avoid old Dan, who had strict orders not to let us "tumble in," and who dogged our footsteps like fate.

"Dan!" said I, "there's the squire calling" (Dan was a little deaf). "Don't you hear him?"

Mary looked at me with wondering eyes, and listened too.

"I don't hear your grandpapa calling, Terence," she said, quietly.

"Ah! but I do, Mary. There! there! he's shouting for you, Dan." And as the old fellow, after waiting a minute with his hand to his ear, caught in the hollow of it the rumble of the breeze, and started off, I whispered, laughingly— "Now, you see, he's gone. The squire's ever so far away, and we'll have five minutes to ourselves. Come along this way."

"And the squire didn't call?" asked Mary, as she drew herself up, and threw back her head, and stared me full in the face. " Do you mean to say, Terence, you've told—a fib?" she gasped.

" Why, Mary, it's only out of fun—only to make old Dan run away, and to be able to bring you quite close to the water to show you something. Come till you see," and I held out my hand.

But she was gone; flying as fast as her little legs could carry her after Dan, and sobbing out, " Oh! wicked, wicked Terry, to tell such a fib!" as she flew.

I was astonished, and stood still for a moment; but as Dan was now coming back for me I trotted along the path, little caring for his menacing fist in the air and his scolding for my " thricks;" and striving in vain to make friends with Mary, who, with averted face, kept close to my grandfather, and seemed only intent on adding to the store of primroses and daisies in her lap. There was an expression of deep sorrow and pity on her little face, and when after a time I asked—" Do, Mary, please do make friends with me!" she replied, "No! —not till you have said your prayers to-night and have shown you are sorry for telling a fib like that, Terence!"   What a hard-hearted moralist she was, and how sorry I felt she had such strict views, as it quite spoiled a series of the splendid jokes I intended to practise with her assistance.   That was a very bitter day to me; and when my grandfather, halting for a moment to exhibit a fish he had caught, exclaimed—

"Why, Terry! you and Mary are as quiet as mice; what's the matter with you, children?"

I felt my face glow with a tingling blush as I stammered—

"Mary's cross with me for something, and wont play with me!"

"Eh!—Mary cross?   Why, it's you who look more like cross than she does!   What is this all about?" exclaimed the old gentleman, pausing in the act of changing a fly, and scrutinizing us through his spectacles—"Has he been teasing you, my dear?"

"Oh! no, indeed, dear Doctor!" she said, with her arms folding her apron full of flowers to her heart, so that her face just surmounted the heap— "Terence hasn't teased me at all.   He is very good and kind—that is, he meant it for fun, and to please me—Oh, sir!" she cried, suddenly clasping her hands together, and letting all the flowers tumble to her feet, " don't be angry—but Terence vexed me because he told a fib—he's sorry now, I'm sure, and he'll promise never to do it again if you forgive him. Wont you, Terry?" she added, turning on me a look of entreaty I can recollect as if it were yesterday.

" A-fib !—hem—a fib !" quoth my grandfather, with a " March-brown" between his fingers; " that is indeed very wrong. What was it ? More white than black, I hope. Come, as you have begun you must go on with it, Mary, you know. Perhaps it's a hanging matter, and in that case we can march the culprit off at once !" he added, with an odd look about his face, " for I'm a magistrate, you know."

Miss Mary Butler, with some hesitation of speech, and a few glances at me, which said very plainly she was sorry for me but must do her duty, then laid before his worship with minute detail the whole of my monstrous wickedness. I felt guilty to the soles of my feet ; I dared not look up.

" Although I told him I did not hear you calling before Dan began to run," she concluded.

" Phew !" whistled the Doctor, softly ; " was ever a more terrible case than this ? I wonder where this dreadful boy got such naughty ideas, and where on earth, my dear Mary, you were taught such a love of truth?   Not at the castle, I'll be bound.   No, indeed—no, indeed," he said, putting his hand over her dark curls; " from Nature, my child.   You are your mother's true daughter, and she had a monopoly of the good qualities of half your house, at all events.   And now," he continued, turning to me, " you see, Terry, how you have disgraced yourself!   You can only be sorry now, and promise to tell no more fibs ; but there is no use in doing that unless you mean to keep your word."

Was I not very sorry?   And was I not very glad when Mary took my hand and asked me not to be angry with her, " because she could not help it."

Many a day has that scene on the Carra returned to me, and I have smiled at the recollection of everything about it except my little companion's gravity, and the earnestness of her face, and the great contentment of heart when all was at an end.   The lesson was too slight and the matter too trifling to cause a deeper impression ; and my grandfather's twinkling eye and smiling mouth told me I had done no great harm after all.

The old mansion, which was dignified by the name of Bradystown House, and a few hundred acres of what looked like a remanet from the deluge—for a duck might consider it land and a hen might regard it as water—were all that remained to the family (of which my grandfather declared he was the head in those parts) of a good slice of the county that had once been theirs. The house was a great block of red brick, with stone copings and a stucco portico, to which an extremely unfinished look was given by a small wing at one side, which the last of the O'Bradys had not lived —or indeed, had he lived, would not have had the money—to complete. The edifice was only commenced in the beginning of the last century, after the " castle" had been destroyed by a lieutenant of De Ginkel, on his march to the Shannon, in order to punish the owner, who had joined King James. The ruins of the castle were near at hand, and a portion of them served to close in the garden walls, and were useful as cellars and as winter-sheds for cattle.

The house stood on a gentle elevation amid a few old trees, in which a scanty array of faithful rooks still found refuge, unseduced by the ampler accommodation of the woods around the residence of Sir Richard Desmond. Before the windows an ill-kempt lawn, given up to pasturage, which rejoiced in the title of "The demesne," gradually melted into the waters of the lough, that spread away till it merged in the " Bay of Carra" on one side, and on the other opening into a series of large pools, received the waters of the river, draining the higher ridges of a great range of hills, on a spur of which the architect had raised the family mansion. There was little, indeed, of the land which belonged to us that a farmer would have called " land" at all. All the good acreage had gone bit by bit; sometimes the bits were very large. Sir Richard's drainage operations had delivered his fields of the water, which was accorded so liberally to ours that it would be hard to believe there was a drop of moisture left on his farms. A few wretched peasants held their little patches of moor, rather as tenants by courtesy of the landlord than by any monetary acknowledgment of their obligations as occupants of arable and pasturage. Their dwellings, scattered over the bog amid patches of green, which marked the reclaimed land —or rather, the soil not yet gone to waste—were like huge manure heaps or exaggerated ant-hills : brown tumuli without form, but by no means void, for each of the tenants would have thought himself poor indeed if he had not a family of many children, to be used as so many arrows in his quiver when doing battle with "the masther" or the agent about an imaginary payment of rent.

And how had all this come about ?　Well, it is a long story, and it took some hundreds of years to furnish the materials for it.　But in effect the latter part of the tale was this :—

Maurice O'Brady, by marriage with one of the Desmonds in the later days of Elizabeth, managed to recover the smallest of the estates which his father had forfeited by his forced complicity in O'Neil's rebellion.　He was sent abroad when a child, to be made a good Catholic; but in his wanderings, ere he was of age, he had sojourned at the university of Prague, and had distinguished himself after a time by his physical zeal in the tumults which arose between the orthodox and the new lights of the time on the side of the latter, so that his father, who was living in seclusion and *making his soul* among the friars of the Irish Benedictines at Paris, took much comfort to himself that he had no lands left for such a reprobate Hussite and heretic to enjoy.　But a little later, when Maurice, joining the Imperialists, gained a name for himself as a brave soldier, to which in a few years he added the reputation of a skilful captain, the old man rejoiced that his son was fighting like a good Catholic Christian after all ; and bemoaned the evil fortunes of his house and the cowardice of the kernes, which had given Essex such easy victories, and left the O'Bradys of Lough-na-Carra nothing but bitter memories and broken fortunes. When his father died, Maurice's heritage was a small sum of money and a solemn entreaty that he would return to his native country.

"Do not let the name die out. If we all go, it is what the enemy want. We must be politic, Maurice—be politic, and watch and wait. If the lion sees the hunter he will kill him; but if the hunter is wary, watches, and waits, the beast is his at last."

A friend of Sidney, whom Maurice saved in a sudden rout of the Christians by the banks of the Leytha, repaid him by obtaining grace and pardon for the offence of being an impenitent rebel's son. Nay, the Lord Deputy himself did not hesitate to express his opinion, that Captain Maurice Brady might render good service to his royal mistress if only he were taken into her gracious favour, as he was a gentleman of conduct and courage, with a fitting sense of the errors of his unhappy father, and in no way to be regarded as a " Papist enemy." In fact, Maurice Brady, who at this time made his name a dissyllable, was even permitted to appear at the court of the Queen; and, in two years after his return, was fortunate enough to marry a younger daughter of one of the Desmonds, among the most powerful of the old families of the Pale. Two years later a grant —not without much outcry from the Irish Parliament —put him in possession of a share of his family estates. It was understood that Maurice Brady was almost as good as a Protestant, and that he only waited for a fair occasion to declare it to the world. But the occasion never came; and by his neighbours of Norman and English descent he was regarded as little better than a common Irish traitor. Living among a barbarous people, or at least a race whose civilization he did not understand, and whose language was unknown to him, the travelled soldier became overwhelmed with *ennui*. There was more than a suspicion that he was cognizant of the Irish rising in the reign of James; and Maurice, whose wife had died after giving birth to an only son, sailed from Galway to a Spanish port, leaving his heir in the care of his brother-in-law; and re-entering the Imperialist service, was killed in the decisive charge at the battle of the White Mount.

Terence, his son, was brought up in the traditions of the Desmonds, and was educated in England. After a boisterous youth, he married a lady of the house of the Lucys of Warwickshire, and fell in the Civil War, fighting, with the perversity of his race, for the King.

Of his two sons and three daughters none ever saw the land of their ancestors except one, Gerald, the second son, who, through the exertions of his English friends, got possession of Lough-na-Carra and Kilmoyle at the close of the reign of Charles II. Gerald subsequently showed his gratitude by joining the Royalists at the summons of Tyrconnel, a few days before the arrival of James in Ireland, and his judgment by the loss of his lands. He was one of the garrison of Limerick, and died in exile in France; and it was not till the reign of Anne that his elder brother, who joined the winning side and the victorious faith, was rewarded by the restoration of a small portion of the land of Lough-na-Carra, and the ruins of the old castle. But Miles Brady had married an heiress, and he resolved to build a fine house in the midst of his people, whom he proposed to civilize, having all that faith in

Saxonizing the Celts which has done so little good, and so much evil, in time past. His efforts were not successful; his money and his time went in vain. He found a stiff-necked generation, whose ways were not his ways; and after a few weary years of toil, he left his tenants unconverted and his house unfinished; returned to England in disgust, became one of an active knot of Whig pamphleteers and wits, who met in a coffee-house near Lincoln's Inn Fields; wrote many forgotten papers; engaged in many broils and squabbles; and died of a wound received in a street quarrel, coming out of Drury Lane.

It was an unlucky house; what one of them gained the next was sure to lose; not one of the line for years had been brought up in his own country, or had any feelings or sympathies with his own people. They drew as much money as they could get, and spent it. What else could a gentleman do, unless he were a rebel? And no one in those days could tell what loyalty or treason was till the definition had been sharply drawn by the sword, or by the decision of the majority (represented by the force) of the people on the other side of the Channel.

My grandfather, Dr. Terence Brady, succeeded

to all that was left of the ever-diminishing estates of Lough-na-Carra, on the death of his uncle, and during one of those terrible visitations of typhus which in the old time did the work now performed by emigration, and in its own way checked the increase of population, was summoned from his modest practice as a Dublin physician to deal with a pauper, disaffected population. After his wife fell a victim to the pestilence he only redoubled his exertions, and found a solace for his sorrows in seeking to mitigate the sufferings of others, and in the care of his infant son.

When the rebels of '98 laid waste the houses of the gentry they respected Lough-na-Carra; and the Doctor's loyalty was rather doubted at Dublin Castle when they heard the "Croppies" had not only spared Dr. Brady's house, but had insisted on carrying him on their shoulders from the village— where they found him attending on a dying man— and mounted guard on his gate till they moved off to join the main body of the insurgents. There was not wanting evidence, however, that he had urged them, with tears in his eyes, to desist; and had, unarmed in the midst of their leaders, warned them of their failure and their fate. I can fancy he was eloquent; and I know, indeed, that he was asked to take his place in the Irish Parliament by men who believed his abilities would have secured him a commanding position in political life. But he was fond of his books and of the country, and of doing good, the results of which he could see with his own eyes. The great object of his life was to get Lough-na-Carra into order for his son, who entered the army at the age of sixteen. One sad day the postboy stopped " the Doctor's gig" on the road, and gave him a letter with a great black seal. My grandfather, driving back to the house, and walking into the hall, said calmly to his old housekeeper—

" He's gone! My poor son! The widow and her infant are coming here to their only home. They are on their way now. My darling Jack! To die in an Indian jungle! It is hard, indeed, to bear. But God's will be done!"

I have heard that from the day the news came he was a changed man; but I cannot fancy he could have ever been more gentle, more kind, or more cheerful than he was as I remember him.

CHAPTER II.

AT HOME.

It was some months after this that a postchaise
drove up to the door of the " Desmond Arms," in the
town of Kilmoyle, an event which excited no small
sensation in that very unflourishing place. Not that
the postchaise was a novelty—or the horses or the
postboy—for every one knew Mrs. Dempsey's "quality
carriage"—the Roman-nosed, high-boned steeds,
had a world-wide reputation for their prowess in
kicking, biting, and jumping, and were popularly believed to have been discharged from the mail-coach
service for an inveterate habit of galloping, and
" ould Pat," the postboy, was better known than
any milestone on the turnpike road—but that the
occupants of the vehicle seemed worthy of much
popular wonder. The first and most attractive of
these was a woman—at least the current opinion
was in favour of the belief that the person in ques-

tion was a female—with a dark-brown face and white teeth, and a small nose on which there was a streak of yellow paint. Through the straight belt of black curls which escaped from the folds of a monster turban of white and red, were visible two massive ear-rings ; a thin white and scarlet jacket, looped at the neck, permitted a large extent of dark skin to be seen in the region of the breast, under which the jacket was gathered in by a thick shawl folded round the waist, and thence emerging came down to the knees. As the owner of the curls and ear-rings stepped out of the carriage, the multitude, which consisted by this time of at least two-thirds of Kilmoyle, who were old or young enough to run, and who were within half a mile of the "Desmond Arms," beheld with amazement and delight, below the short white drawers completing the stranger's costume, a pair of small brown bandy legs and large brown flat feet, on the little toes of which were two silver rings ; and their excitement was at its height when a roll of white linen which was borne tenderly in the arms of the strange being emitted a shrill cry, as like that of a Christian baby as any the many matrons there familiar with the sound had ever heard. That cry was uttered by me, Terence Brady, awakened out of a very comfortable sleep, no doubt by Mohun's descent to the earth from the postchaise. The emotions aroused among the crowd by the utterance might have led to an instant demand for my exposure to the air, but that a huge ape, with a silver collar and chain round his neck, which had been asleep in a corner of the carriage, made his appearance on the steps, and grinning round him, and puckering up his face, surrounded by a fringe, and beard of long grey hair and sunken yellow eyes, gave a sharp whimper, and with a bound rushed after the dark stranger, jumped upon his back—for it was a he—and, with one arm round his neck, chattered defiance at the people of Kilmoyle.

The diversion was most effective, and as soon as the novel visitors were lost sight of in the passage of the inn, the popular mind was agitated by tremendous doubts on the question of identity, for the postboy assured the crowd that the party consisted of " poor Captain Brady's widdy, nurse, and child ;" and that they had been given to his charge by the guard of the mail-coach from Cork, with a strict injunction to take particular care of the nurse, who was the hairy lady with the silver collar.

" I saw the child's face, anyway, and it's as white as my own,"—an illustration, by-the-bye, of no special note in regard to whiteness—" and I don't know how the poor Ingin widdy can be the mother, for she's as black as soot. But they've quare ways in foreign parts."

My grandfather, who had been long expecting our coming, as always happens in such cases, was taken by surprise at the message that the " captain's little son and two strange Indian gentlemen had arrived."   He smiled sadly as he was pulling on his boots, and exclaimed—

" Do you take poor Mrs. Brady for a gentleman, Pat ?"

" Begorrah, yer honour, all I can say is I've seen thim all; and if there's a lady among them she's as much hair on her face as Serjint Quin, at the dippo in Athlone."

When Doctor Brady, scarcely noticing the remark, entered the room in the " Desmond Arms," he stood as much aghast as any of the people of the village.

Mohun, squatted on the floor with a large basin between his knees, was carefully washing me from head to foot; and having taken off his turban, the better to get at his work, his curly black hair had fallen down on his face and shoulders, nearly obscuring his features, but not hiding the large rings in his ears.   His loose white dress had all the appearance of a woman's robe, and his diminutive stature confirmed the idea which took possession of my grandfather's mind for a moment, when he observed a still smaller individual seated on a chair before the looking-glass, with a huge head-dress, a pair of horn spectacles, and a cloud of drapery on its person.

"Good God!" thought he, as he told his friends when he narrated the story, "did my poor son marry a native woman after all?   And is this the creature who is my daughter-in-law!"

In fact, Jacko, who was more sedate than most of his race and genus, had put on Mohun's turban, encased himself in my toggery without much discrimination of the proper uses of each little garment, put on the glasses which Mrs. Dempsey had left lying on her book when she was disturbed by our advent, and was examining the general effect in the mirror; so that the horrid notion flashed on the Doctor that Mohun was my mother, and that the ape, whose physiognomy he could not well catch as it sat with its back turned on him in the chair, was a privileged attendant.

"Where is the lady?—where is my daughter-in-law?" he inquired as he glanced round the room.

Mohun, who was drying me, and putting on a fresh set of clothes, which he took from one of the portmanteaus that had come over in the post-chaise, had by this time gathered up his locks, and got his head into his turban. He looked cautiously around him, and sidling towards my grandfather, held me out in both hands.

"Dis de leetl sahib—de only one I have, sir—me and Derry sahib and de black rascal dare—all that come, sahib, surela."

"Where is your mistress?—Where is Mrs. Brady? What do you mean by all that confounded gibberish?"

Mohun deposited me·gently on a chair. Then unwinding his sash very slowly, he opened its folds, took out a piece of oilskin, cut the strings around it, and showed my grandfather a letter.

"De sahib is Brady sahib's father?" he inquired. "Dis chitty for him."

"Of course I am—of course it is," cried the Doctor, as he seized the letter, and broke the black seal. He had only read a few lines ere he uttered an exclamation of surprise, and crumpled the letter in his hands.

"My God!—is it possible? What a heartless wretch," he moaned, "what a fate!"

My grandfather buried his face in his hands, and then, after a pause, walked over to the easy chair in which I had been deposited, and taking me tenderly in his arms, whilst the tears rolled down his face, kissed me gently, and repeated to himself—

"Take charge of my dear child! Yes! indeed I will, my poor little waif, thus drifted to this barren shore.   As long as I live my son's son shall be my only thought.   It is incredible! It is quite beyond belief! And yet he must have loved her—"

Jacko had got hold of the letter, and was opening it with much precision and curiosity, fold after fold, when my grandfather suddenly made a rush at him, shouting out—

"Drop it, you thief!—drop it!"

Which Jacko certainly would not have done if Mohun, who with folded arms had stood motionless hitherto, scanning the Doctor's face narrowly, had not joined in the chase, and compelled the surrender of the document.

"You will take your young master over in the carriage. The luggage will go in the cart under the charge of one of the servants, and your hairy friend there. I will be over before you, and have a nurse to look after the child."

He took the letter into the back parlour of the inn. It was half an hour ere he emerged with an air which was very different from his usual genial, contented aspect.

"The Doctor's fretting agen about the captain, and seeing the grandson has brought him back to it," remarked Mrs. Dempsey. "Or maybe it's the suddin news coming on him of the poor crachure that's drownded. It's hardships he has to bear wid, the poor man. And to be left wid a child a year old, and that black hagger of a Turk, and the other thing on him, is enough to dhrive him mad. The Lord pity and look down on him this day!"

And so the story of my orphanage was known ere the details of the escape of the *Ross-shire* from total wreck, and the account of the calamity, by which twenty-three persons were lost in the swoop of that deadly wave on her decks, got into the newspapers.

All I knew of my father was, that he was a tall man, with dark eyes, which followed me from the wall as I went round the room—light hair, cut short; small whiskers, coming to an abrupt ending on a line with the point of his nose; that he wore a scarlet coat with large silver epaulettes, tight lemon-coloured pantaloons with embroidered frogs, and highly shining boots. There he stood, leaning one hand on the hilt of a most formidable curved sabre. In the other he held a pair of gloves and a plumed shako, his back turned on a very fierce engagement on the side of a very blue mountain besmirched with the smoke of a burning city, in which elephants, camels, black men in white dresses, and white men in red dresses, were fighting, whilst a highly philosophical native held a champing charger, in case the fortunes of the combat were decided against Captain Brady's detachment, which, however, succeeded in routing the famous Pindarry, Poll Sing, and storming his stronghold.

There were, too, some memorials of him beside those of the Calcutta artist—tiger-skins with bullet-marks into which I pushed my fingers, stuffed birds, Indian curiosities, and models of forts, and, most treasured of all, framed and glazed over the fire-place, the despatches in which his name was honourably recorded, and the " order of the day" in which he was promoted for good service and bravery in the field.

My grandfather rather diminished my great

interest in this portrait by saying as I was gazing upon it one day—

"You must not think, Terry, that is very like your father. He had not that stern look—at least as I used to see him;—he was not so cross. And he had beautiful hands and feet; his eyes were brighter and softer. But still there's some look of him; you could just know him by the picture, that's all."

"And is that very like poor mamma, grandpapa?" inquired I, with an assurance that he would say "yes." My faith in the picture of my father had gone at once.

"Well, my dear child, I can't tell you. You know I never saw her; your father married in India. But Major Turnbull at the Castle who came over to talk to me of my poor son, whose great friend he was, said it was a very good likeness indeed, but that no artist in India— he doubted, indeed, if any in the world—could do full justice to the wonderful beauty which made all his comrades envy poor Jack, and think him the luckiest fellow in the world at first——"

"Why at first, grandpapa? Didn't they always think him so?"

My grandfather stammered a little as he said, looking me full in the face—

" Your mother did not enjoy—very good health. It is expensive to be sick in India; that's all."

As I looked—I often did—on the lovely face which the painter—a better hand probably than the artist who had essayed to depict my father—had succeeded in endowing with an expression of the most charming sweetness and simplicity, I was happy to think that there at least I might rely on having a faithful resemblance of one of those I could never see on this earth.

My mother was half-reclining on a couch, with one hand hidden in a wild labyrinth of golden-coloured hair, whilst another caressed a spotted creature which my nurse told me was a young tiger, but which I knew afterwards to be an ocelot, one of the most graceful and sleek of the beautiful cruel cat tribe. The dark hues of the creature's skin, as, with half-closed eyes, it made believe to bite her tiny fingers, set off· the snowy whiteness of her arm. The white robe in which she was enveloped was confined by a gold girdle at the waist, and fell in easy folds over a form of exquisite symmetry, leaving a glimpse of one fairy foot in a gorgeous slipper, peeping beneath; the other a marvel of smallness, hung slipperless over the edge of the sofa, as if the tiny covering had been kicked off in a pet, or carelessly let drop on the carpet. The eyes, full of dreamy abstraction, seemed looking into space—a blue which had a tinge of violet, shaded by a long fringe of lashes darker than her hair, and matching the lines of her brown eyebrows; an upper lip curved, slightly parted, and displaying the white teeth, was set over its firmer, straighter fellow, as though she were sighing gently, or uttering some word of endearment to her spotted plaything; while from the tanglement of her hair one taper finger had stolen and rested at the angle of her mouth.

The whole character of the attitude was one of indolent repose. By her side, on the ground, lay an opened book, which had fallen on some flowers, the leaves of which littered the rich carpet; and the rays of the setting sun creeping in through an opening in a lattice, lighted up the countenance and figure of one who seemed to me beautiful and bright as an angel reclining in some fairy bower, where the richest stuffs and gold and silver sheen formed a background of indescribable magnificence. I had gazed, when I was young, on those eyes till I fancied they kindled with a responsive glance; had babbled away to "dear mamma" till I thought some fond word came from her half-opened lips. Often had I mounted on a chair, and with a thousand little wiles sought to attract the notice of those great blue orbs, or embraced the cold flat canvas; but I bore to the young tiger a hate that once led me to begin an attack on him with a stick, which was only prevented at the outset by the vigilant Honour.

In fact, there was an altar in that frame on which I made my sacrifices of love and affection to a mother's memory. If I dreamt of angels they appeared to me like my mother, and in my infant prayers I was wont to sigh that I might soon be taken to her and lie in her bosom.

Whenever any childish grief came upon me, I stole into the gloomy old room, which was seldom used then, for the days of grand dinner parties were over, and made her image my confidant—addressed to her my tearful sorrows, and pressed my lips to the placid brow till it warmed to their touch. The portrait was my ideal of all that was perfection and goodness—of all that was pure and beautiful; and often in the dark I lay awake, gazing into the black void, till the fiery specks which danced about before my eyes faded away, and there the gracious form in its robe of white floated in the air—the eyes and mouth smiled on me; and the faithful Honour, anxious to know why my breath came so fast, shook me from my nightmare, and declared that " the picture was bewitchin' Masther Terry, and that if I didn't lave off, out of the house it must go."

The sad story I had gathered up so eagerly out of many a fragmentary hint, ere I had by incessant questioning obtained all the particulars from the old nurse, was short and pitiful. After my father's death, which took place very suddenly, my mother, who had no rich relatives, set sail for Europe in the *Ross-shire* East Indiaman. The vessel struck on a dangerous reef off the coast of Ceylon. It was in the night time; the ship was crowded with passengers; they rushed up when the crash roused them in their berths; and as they gathered on the quarter-deck a tremendous sea, sweeping from stem to stern, bore many of them into the boiling surf. Among them were my poor mother and her maid.

"Oh! why," I cried, "why was I not taken too? It was cruel to leave me! I, so little worth! And to carry her off to that dreadful death, where her cries were drowned in the howling

·of the wind, and choked by the wicked waters, as her fair limbs were dashed against the harsh sharp rocks." She and her companions in that sudden misery were never seen again. The stout ship was driven by another sea with her bow on a ridge of coral, and lay for many hours dismasted and help-less; but the gale, which was failing when the vessel struck, abated; the sea fell, a sail was fastened under the leak, and the *Ross-shire* was carried in a sinking state into Galle harbour. Transferred into another ship, Mohun and Jacko and I were, after many adventures, in which the two former played distinguished parts, safely de-posited, as we have seen, in the " Desmond Arms."

As I grew up I became aware that there was a tenderness and compassion in the tone of all around me, from my dear grandfather down to the turf-boy and peasant girls, who overcame their horror and fear of Mohun and his ape sufficiently to approach my little open car when I was driven out in state by Pat with my two dark attendants; which for a long time I thought was natural. I was spoilt by constant petting and sympathy, which I could not understand. My only great trouble was caused by Mohun, who led a very uncom-fortable life in his new home, and who found new discomforts every year. He was a Christian, he said, and as good a Roman Catholic as any in the parish. But Father Drennan, the parish priest, declared he was next to a heretic. Father Driver, the coadjutor, protested he was worse than a heathen. Mohun's religious notions were founded, in fact, on the compromise between Hindooism and Christianity, which is taken sometimes by missionaries to represent native conversion. He obstinately refused to go to confession; and after a few Sundays he cut off a great treat to the whole population by ceasing to attend mass, because he said the " white budmashes" stared at him, and pulled off his turban; and the validity of his excuses was admitted the more readily by the Doctor in consequence of the devilish pranks which Jacko played in the house during his absence.

" He would not ate his m'ails like a Christian," said the servants. Mohun sat apart with his head uncovered, crouched on the floor over his heap of rice, cooked with his own hands, closely watched by his bunder, to whom he gave handfuls now and then. He wore beads, but he did not count them in a proper manner. Biddy Hennessy, the dairymaid, had been obliged on one occasion to give him what she called " a regular lambasthin," in consequence of his " offering" to kiss her, and in that respect, and in a partiality for whisky, lay the only traits, all the people declared, in which he resembled a Christian at all.   At intervals letters came for him, and then he would sit for hours writing strange characters on thin paper, and he posted with his own hands the heavy envelopes, on which the only word the postmistress could make out was " Bombay," with postage of fabulous amount.   He spent little money except on rolls of white and coloured calico, which he made into clothing with his own hands; and when he received his wages, he changed his small roll of notes at the village store for. silver. Where he stowed it none could guess, but he lent out money now and then on heavy usury to the people round the place; and the popular dislike to him was aggravated by the sharpness of his bargains, and the exactness of his accounts.

One day the postman brought a letter for Mohun, and my grandfather was trying to decipher the direction, on which some words in English had fixed his attention, when the Madrassee, with his usual noiseless step, approached, and stood for a moment with bowed head and arms on his breast, till the Doctor handed it to him with the remark—

"This letter has just come with mine. I was thinking I had seen that handwriting before. Can I be right? Do you get letters from her, Mohun?"

Mohun took the letter, and thrust it into his breast.

"Dat chitty come from my wife, sahib," he replied. "No oder mem sahib write Mohun chittys."

"I don't believe you, Mohun," replied my grandfather. "I long have had my suspicions. Let me take that letter to Major Turnbull at the Castle, and see if you speak the truth."

Mohun's voice trembled a little as he said—"Mohun beg Doctor sahib not to ask him. Him wife not like her chitty to be read by Major Trumble, or anyone but Mohun."

"Then," retorted my grandfather, angrily—"I tell you, the sooner you go back to your real mistress the better. I will have no one here whom I don't trust. No spies; do you hear? Master Terence can do very well without you, so you had better prepare to go back to your own country. The sooner the better."

Mohun bowed meekly — "I go when Doctor please. Jacko not very well in him health. Mohun was thinking some time since he would ask Doctor to have him both go back.   He will be very sorry to leave him Master Derry, but he soon forget poor Mohun."

And so I did.   The attachments of youth do not bear great strain.   There was a sort of barrier between Mohun and myself, which thickened as time wore on.   He avoided direct anwers to my endless questions about my mother; he knew nothing more than all the world knew; he had not lived long with the Captain before his death and the voyage to Europe.   Nevertheless I persecuted Mohun, asking him for ever about the event, and always hearing the same story of the storm, the striking ship, the rush to the deck, the sweep of the great wave, the awful cry of agony as through the black night struggling figures in white were borne away into the raging surf.   "Master Derry—poor mamma! de ayah, Bengalee woman— O, many ayahs, many sahibs, and de mate and sahiblogue and littel child all gone away!" and at last Mohun got cross.   I had never seen the sea; I looked through all the books I could find for pictures of ships, and presented Mohun with engravings of Raphael's cartoon of "The Miraculous Draught of Fishes"—of a Roman galley —of "Our Saviour walking on the Water"—of

Noah's ark : all in vain. "Not like dat big ship—not same as dat, Master Derry."

One day Major Turnbull happened to ride over from the Castle to see my grandfather on business, and as he dismounted I ran out to see his famous Arab charger. Whilst the Major stood for a moment in the hall, Mohun came in search of me, and the Major spoke to him in a strange language. I, who was accustomed to every expression of that mysterious dark face, saw that Mohun was agitated. He trembled, indeed, as he replied ; and when I saw the Major raising his riding-whip in a menacing way, I ran to him, and said imploringly—"Oh, dear Major Turnbull, don't be angry with poor Mohun ; I love him very much, and so does grandpapa."

The Doctor just at the moment came out to welcome his friend, and as they walked away together to the study, I heard the Major say—

"Why, Brady, you told me the black fellow who came over with the little boy was a Madrassee."

"And so he is, I believe ; at least he says so, if I understood him right."

"Not a bit of it ; no more a Madrassee than I am. Some up-country fellow, and inclined to be deuced cheeky.   A scamp from Delhi or Agra, I should think.   And what the deuce——"

I heard no more, as the door shut; but when I said to Mohun, "The Major says you're not a Madrassee, but a scamp from the up-country, Delhi or Agra," Mohun looked troubled, and mumbled out, "Master Derry, dear! Major sahib tink all we tell lies. He know better dan me where I come from.   Ho! ho!"

Somehow or other this little thing made an impression on me, and I felt that Mohun had not spoken the truth.   The stories told by the servants created almost as great a fear of the Hindoostanee as that which had long ago been inspired in me by Jacko.   That remarkable creature had been indisposed for some time, and had literally taken to his bed.   Mohun placed his room at his disposal, and Jacko, who was of a chilly nature, lay for hours under the blankets, with his face just visible, and one long hairy arm out on the floor, languidly raising the dainties Mohun left within his reach to his pursed-up lips.   The servants declared that in the dead of night Mohun and the ape held long conversations together in a "kind of Frinch;" and a daring pantry-boy protested that he had seen the Indian and Jacko seated at table one night, drinking hot whisky-punch and smoking tobacco, "just like two Christians." And so this poor fellow, who had nursed and tended me — on whose neck I had hung for years—whose dark cheeks I had so often kissed—and who had lulled me to sleep with songs, the strains of which still float through my memory —who had rejoiced in my joy, and soothed my infant sorrows — left Lough-na-Carra for ever, as little regretted as if he were a passing stranger.

When Mohun went—it was a memorable day—I felt rather glad than sorry, and my conscience reproached me for my indifference. The little man had collected all his property—two large bags, and his cooking pots and pans as bright as silver—in the back hall; Jacko, carefully dressed in a scarlet frock, with a large piece of flannel wrapped round his chest, sat between them, munching an apple, and coughing " just like a Christian," whilst his eyes followed all his master's motions. The chaise was drawn up outside to take the party to the mail-coach, and the servants stood in a group to see them off. Mohun came down from my grandfather, who was confined to his room by a cold, and the girdle fastened round his waist seemed heavier than ever. He bade all the servants " Good-bye" in his own fashion, and to the astonishment of each, he offered as a parting gift a small gold piece, which produced rather a favourable impression.

"Faith, Misther Mohun's not so bad, afther all," exclaimed the cook, Biddy Flynn.

"Maybe he'd take ye off to Ingy wid him av ye axed him. He's his own cook, and ye'd have light work of it, Biddy," chuckled Honour.

"Bedad, maybe it's tin black wives I'd find at home wid him. Ax him yourself, Miss Honner."

Mohun was very grave. "Master Derry, dear Master Derry, some day you know who Mohun keep him rupee for," said he; "Mohun got little, very little rupee; but he not keep dem for himself." The fellow drew me towards him, and as he put his arms round my neck and kissed me, a tear trickled over his cheek. "Honna, you take care of Master Derry. You not let him burn himself, Honna; nor fall into the river, Honna; nor get drown like him mudder. Master Derry dear, some day you ask your granfader tell you how Mohun's missis was drown. He will tell you some day." Again he kissed me, mumbled some words in a tongue I did not understand, and summoning Jacko, who blinked, wheezed, and coughed at the exertion of getting into the post-chaise, drove off with his eyes fixed on me, amid a chorus of

"Good-bye, Misther Mohun!—good-bye, Jacko!—
God send yez safe to Injy!" and a parting injunction from the cook to the postboy to "Mind them
two black gintlemen, and carry them safe to the
coach."

This is a long episode; but I fear there is no
regularity, no order, in this rambling, stumbling
history, which rarely goes off at score, but which
halts and kicks, or even insists on backing in a most
wilful, unbroken, and provoking manner. I am
coming to a great epoch in this part of my life.
Up to this time I was nearly as happy as boyhood
can be. There were no wants I could not gratify
—there was no craving for anything I could not
obtain. I did not feel the need of playmates, for
all in my little world were ready to join in any
sport, and I was in the proud position of being
the director of my own pastimes. Now and then
indeed came moments of reverie, when I thought
of her I had lost—the sunshine vanished, and darkness came upon me. But the sadness did not
endure long—the clouds soon passed away. My
grandfather's care stood in lieu of the father's solicitude and the mother's affection which I had
never known. Orphan I was indeed, but I was
proud to feel I was the son of a gallant soldier; and

if my tears flowed as I sat with clasped hands before my mother's image, there was in my sorrow more of pity than of pain.   So might it have been till time had done its work.   But it was not to be. Far better is it ever to let the young know all that concerns them, than torture them with mysteries and deceit at the very time when curiosity is most lively and the character most susceptible of permanent impressions.

CHAPTER III.

It was one evening long after Mohun's departure from Lough-na-Carra.

"It is a very curious thing, my dear doctor, that you never could get an exact account of the loss of your daughter-in-law among those people on board the ship."   The speaker was Sir Richard Desmond, and I heard the words just as, in all the glories of my finest clothes, I was introduced, or rather butted, into the dining-room by Honour, with my hair "done up," and a face brought to the highest degree of polish.   There was a little dinner-party after a hunt.   Sir Richard, and Major Turnbull from the Castle, the Rector of Lough-na-Carra—who never went to hunt, but often "came by" as the hounds were throwing off, so that the Rev. Frank Stack might be seen very much as if he were engaged in the chase, although he was really, he said, only giving his famous mare, Daisy, a canter over the turf in the direction of the run— a couple of officers from Athlone, Mr. Rackstraw, Sir Richard's agent, and two of the neighbouring squires, completed the company; they were all evidently listening with great interest to something which concerned me, for on my appearing at the door, my grandfather said—

"Hush! here he is. Now, Terry, make your best bow, and come sit between me and Sir Richard."

"He's getting very like his father," quoth Major Turnbull; "but he'll hardly be better looking, for poor Jack was a deuced good-looking fellow. What are you going to be, Terry?"

"I should like to be a soldier, sir," replied I, through an interval of my glass of sherry and sweet biscuit.

"There it is, you see," said Sir Richard. "The scarlet fever will skip a generation, but it will come out in the Bradys."

"Yes," sighed my grandfather. "It has been a fatal disease among us. I hope to be able to cure it in this instance. The poor boy will have neither money nor interest, and without either or both soldiering is a bad trade."

"You may say that, sir," exclaimed one of the officers. "Here am I, after all my service, sticking fast among the subs, whilst one fellow after another purchases over me; and as I have no friends to help me, I am likely to remain as I am for years to come, unless there's an epidemic breaks out among the field officers and captains."

"But the army's not as bad as the church," chimed in the Rector. "Here am I for the last twenty years rector of this parish of Lough-na-Carra, and I don't see a chance of promotion."

"Yes, my dear sir," cried Sir Richard; "but then Lieutenant Dashwood joined a service in which he looked for promotion in this world, whilst you will no doubt receive spiritual preferment in another."

"And as it is, Stack," added Mr. Rackstraw, "eight hundred a year, a good house, and the glebe lands of Kilmoyle, put you on the level with lucky general officers at least. You don't often meet a fellow in the king's service who is a general in the space of twenty-eight years."

"All this has nothing to do with my young friend, Terry," said the Major; "you will set him wondering whether he can put any trust in what he hears at church, if you let him think money is the only object a man should look to in life."

"I am sure I don't teach him that lesson," remarked my grandfather; "and if I did, he would soon perceive my practice was different from my precept.   He has already accused me of not giving him a chance of being a good boy, because I have never given him a flogging, for he knows the Bible says 'Spare the rod and spoil the child.'"

"And of course you told him," said the Rector, "that it meant, if the boy who deserved the rod did not get it, he was likely to be spoiled; and Terry does not deserve it."

I confess I had my own opinion on that subject, being aware of divers circumstances for which a little chastisement might have been duly administered; but I kept it to myself.   The conversation got on to subjects in which I had no interest, and which I did not understand, about church and state and the army, whilst I was burning to tell them all the reasons why I wanted to be a soldier; I wished to have a scarlet coat and gold lace, and ride a splendid horse, like Colonel Brady, of the King of Spain's service, whose picture was in the hall, or wear a silver cuirass and helmet, like Field-Marshal Graf von Bradé, who was depicted over the mantelpiece, seated on a champing steed, truncheon in hand, directing the charge of his squadrons against a confused mass of horsemen in turbans. That money had anything to do with all this bravery I never imagined, and I could now only conjecture that the tailors charged a great deal for such fine dresses. When I retired to my little room, under charge of Honour, I sought for information; but my good nurse could not tell me much. "My brither is in the army sojerin, and he's a corplar in the Buffs, and all I know is, though he ses he should be ped more nor a shillin a day, he hasn't got above twopence or a thruppenny bit to bless hisself wid."

"Honny, why doesn't grandfather get what Sir Richard calls an exact account of the loss of poor mamma? Grandfather's daughter-in-law was my mamma, wasn't she?"

"Indeed an she was. Sorra one of me knows, Masther Terry alanna, why they don't know! Shure, how could the docthor get an exact recount from the poor lady, and she at the bottom of the say? People ses Sir Richard has got more money nor brains, though he's making the one fly before the other. And now say yer prayers—and I wish it

4—2

was a pather an' ave, an' prayers that could be of use to you, darlint, yez larned to say—and go to bed."

But every time I looked at the portrait, the thought of Sir Richard's question and the embarrassed air of my grandfather came into my mind. There was something I could not make out in the story I had heard; and it was evident others were also not quite satisfied.

Mohun's parting advice came to my mind. A day or two afterwards my grandfather was in the parlour, and I on a stool at his feet was learning my lessons for " Mister Nolan, the schoolmaster," who came regularly to teach me, "unless he could not cross the ford," when the Carra was flooded! (oh, how I delighted in a rainy day!)—though it was hinted that Mister Nolan's floods were sometimes caused by a drought, which could only be slaked in whisky. The old man was watching me, and I was roused from my reverie by his voice.

" What are you thinking of, Terry? You look very dull to-day. I am afraid you are not attending very much to your grammar. If you don't feel well tell me, and we will have a holiday."

" I was just thinking of poor mamma. Mohun told me to ask you, and that you would tell me some day how she was lost."

" Have you not heard, Terry, over and over again, your mother was drowned ?"

" I have, grandpapa."

" Then why do you ask me ?"

" Because I want to know more, and Mohun said you could tell me."

" Terry, you have heard from Mohun all about the ship, and there is no more for you to know—at least not now, my child."

" Oh, then, there is something I shall know by and by, is there not, dear grandpapa ? Why not tell me now ? I love poor mamma so—some nights I lie awake thinking of her. I love her picture so, and I am sorry God let her be drowned. Oh, grandpapa, do tell me all now."

" My dear child," said my grandfather, with a look which I had seldom seen on his face. " My dear child, you must rest content with what you know already, and you must not ask me these questions again. When you are older you shall hear all I know; and then—then," he added, with a sigh, " my darling Terry, it will not cure your sorrow for your unfortunate mother. Ask me no more. Be content to know she is lost to you and us all."

" Grandfather, I have been reading of divers in

the sea.   Do you think, if I learned to dive, some day, when you tell me all, I could go out and find poor mamma's body?"

"Alas, Terry, the ocean which separates her from you is too deep for any diver. Think no more of this.   You pain your grandfather.   Be patient, and when you know the truth, you will see I was right not to tell it to you now."

" Was her death so very dreadful?"

" Can any death be more painful or dreadful than hers of which you have heard so often ?   I wish that you had not been fascinated by that picture—that you had not seen it yet.   There are things, Terry, more terrible than death.   Now promise me," he said, " you will not open your lips to me about this again till I give you leave.   Good-bye; I am going out for a little drive, and hope to hear a good account of you from Mr. Nolan." And with a fond look and sigh he rose from his chair, patted my head, and kissing my forehead walked out of the room.

But the idea had now begun to haunt me.   There was something more to learn; I could think of nothing else.   When Mr. Nolan came I was lying on the ground before my mother's picture, sobbing as if my heart would break.   The pedagogue could make nothing out of my lessons or out of me, and even the terrors of a bad report to the Doctor did not arouse me to a sense of my pretcrpluperfect of "lego—I read," nor brighten me in "Tarc and Tret." Mr. Nolan was nibbing a pen when my grandfather returned.

"The Muses, Doctor," quoth he, "have deserted our little disciple. Mnemosyne hath fled for the day; and although the ferula be forbidden here, perchance diligence might be stimulated by censure and curtailment of the iligancies of living—sugar, and chrame, and the like of that."

My grandfather had walked over to me, and taking up my arm placed one hand to my wrist and looked at me closely. "Do you feel a head-ache, Terry?"

"I do, grandpapa, just here." There was a throbbing pain and fiery flashes through my eyes.

"Mr. Nolan, I think we will not ask you to come over to-morrow, or till I send Pat across the bog for you. Master Terry is not very well; I find we must make up a little medicine, and give him rest for a few days."

It was long ere I rose from my bed: a fever had declared itself. I remember lights before my eyes, and faces as in a vision—my grandfather's,

Honour's, Mary Butler's; others I did not know. I remember crawling, clammy leeches on my brow, the taste of medicines coming through the disguises of the most favourite jams; I saw in my sick dreams for ever the heavenly figure floating in the air, with blue eyes fixed on mine, and fair hair sweeping over my shoulders, and arched mouth which returned my ardent loving kisses. Will you bear with me and with all my idle memories for awhile? I have met in my life men who have said they never knew an hour's illness, and I pitied them, for if they spoke the truth, they could not have experienced the exquisite pleasure of convalescence, the placid joy of recovering health, the grateful tribute to Self paid by all around the sick bed, which becomes a throne from which the sufferer beholds a household kneeling and paying homage!

But as I lay, with a sort of languid contentment, looking at those who watched me, noting the tenderness of Honour and the ever-growing care of my grandfather, who kicked off his creaky boots in the passage below—stretching my limbs, and now and then baring my sleeve to look at the bony arm and wasted fingers, there was still one thought in my head, "I wonder if grandpapa will tell me when I get well; I must get well and please him, and then perhaps he will keep his promise."

The first morning that I was dressed to make an excursion to another room Honour was delighted.

"Ah, thin! Masther Terry, shure and your breeches is two inches too short for yez. Why, yev grown like Jack and the Bane Stalk. Wirra! wirra! it's new shoots of clothes ye'll have to be gettin' on all sides. It's a regular goint yer become all along of the faver. See here!" she cried to one of the maids; "see here, Katty, if Masther Terry's not a'most as tall as I am, and if he isn't becoming the picture of his mother!"

Katty confirmed Honour on both points. Then came the return of strength, which, like some subtle fluid, slowly filled the body, and the great joy of going downstairs arrived one day at last.

I sat in the sunshine in the porch, till, for very weariness and lack of rest, I begged to be left alone, and asked my grandfather to go out for his daily ride; and then I dosed away in the sunshine, and the face and form of my mother came back again. I left my chair, and with feeble steps tottered through the passage till I came to the door of the old "State Room," and turning the handle I entered, and with eager eyes turned to the accustomed panel. Good heavens! she was not there! The place was vacant; the picture was gone! Ere I could collect my senses, Honour, who had missed me, came into the room, and stood aghast at my face of despair.

"Ah, thin, Masther Terry! is it wantin' to get your death yez are, comin' into the could room out of the sun? Yez ought to be ashamed of yerself; you'll be the death of yer poor grandada, that's done nothin' but watch yez, if the sickness comes on yez again. But what are yez cryin' for, at all at all?"

"Oh, Honny! what have they done with mamma's picture?"

"The picther! An' shure hasn't the Docthor sint it to Dublin to git a tich of varnish, and to have a new frame, as the Injy one was fallin' all to pieces, an' it will be back again afore ye can say Jack Robinson. I wish it nivir cum here, bad cess to it for a picther! I think it's bewitched yez, Masther Terry, shurely."

As I got better, the morbid influence of my illness, or whatever it was, passed away, but still an ever present thought was of my mother. I asked so often about the portrait, that my grandfather confessed it would be a considerable time longer before an artist to whom he had sent it could repair the damage it had sustained by accident on the journey to Dublin.

CHAPTER IV.

THE DISILLUSION.

WHEN I got better, I was asked over to the Castle to spend a few days for change of air and scene. There were ponies to ride and chaises to drive ; there were gardens and orchards ; there was a great pond stocked with fish ; and above all, there was Mary Butler (I had been forgiven long ago for my little fib, and we were the best of friends) to play with whenever her governess, Mdlle. Petitot—whom the country people called " Mamsell Potatoe"—would let her. Sir Richard I seldom saw during the day. There were grand dinners going on. Mary and I, as we were returning from our morning walk or ride, used to meet fine ladies and gentlemen going downstairs to their breakfast, or watched them, still finer, filing in to dinner ere we retired to rest for the night.

One day, as we were seated in the garden in an

arbour, making bouquets out of a large basket of flowers, under the superintendence of "Mamsell Potatoe," we were startled by hearing the voices of people coming towards us along the walk. I could distinguish the tones of Sir Richard and Major Turnbull, mingled with those of ladies laughing and chatting gaily. I rose, shy and awkward, and prepared for flight; but little Mary, turning towards Mam'selle, asked—

"Shall Terry and I go, or shall we stay till uncle comes?"

"Mais pourquoi non, ma chère fille? tu est bien propre—fraîche comme une rose; et le petit Terry, pourquoi va-t-il se cacher quand tout le monde aime le pauvre enfant? Restez donc, tous les deux, chers enfans."

"And here," said Sir Richard, "is one of M'Cracken's pet arbours. He declares it is as good as anything of the kind can be."

The shadows darkened the entrance, and I heard a voice saying,

"Yes, indeed, it is very pretty. And here is my pretty Mary, the most charming flower in the garden, and her little cavalier. Good day, mademoiselle! I envy you the charge you have, and the place of your retreat."

It was my Lady Hautonby who spoke, looking at us through her inseparable glasses, and I felt my cheeks tingle as she went on—" Isn't that Master O'Brady, or O'Grady, very like Gainsborough's ' Blue Boy' ?"

I did not know who or what the "blue boy" was, but I did not like to have the attention of the people, who were all philandering about us, directed specially to myself, and turned away.

" There," she continued, with her dry laugh, " I declare we have got the ' Bashful Irishman' at last. It is only at such an early age the specimen is ever seen; it dies young."

" I suppose it's killed in the ungenial climate it is removed to on transplanting. Our society kills the interesting creature !" joined in one of the gentlemen.

" No, my dear Dolly ! It does not kill; but, like an acid meeting a salt, forms out of it an insipid neutral."

And as they swept on again I caught the words from Sir Richard—

" Did you see how you made your friend, Doctor Brady's little grandson, blush ? He's a sensitive little fellow, and has been very ill lately, and so I have had him over to keep Mary company in her solitude here."

"Kind and unthoughtful as usual, Dick," croaked old Mrs. Gregory, his cousin; "you'll have him and Miss Molly getting up a youthful attachment, and I don't suppose you would approve of the match. I plighted my troth when I was seven years old—didn't I, Dick?"

"My dear Letty! your flirtations began so early —with me, for example—you think such a brilliant commencement is the rule instead of being the exception. I declare we must not talk such folly within the children's hearing. Let us get on, or we shall be late for our ride."

Mary, who had heard every word as well as myself, put her little hand in mine and exclaimed, laughingly—

"Mam'selle, you see Terry and I are to be lovers, and I shall be very fond of him if he doesn't tell any more stories."

But Mam'selle was by no means satisfied with such a pronunciamento; and she said with great severity—

"Mees Maree, a leedle ladie as you should not speak such dings; Master Bradee blush for your indiscreetness of language." At which Mary laughed immensely.

" Why, my dear governess, I have the example of Cousin Letty, and Terry has got the example of Uncle Richard!   You heard what they said."

But Mam'selle only looked at her watch, and with a little scream exclaimed—

" It is dime for Mistere Noland to arrive ! You run off to de study or you shall be late, mon cher petit Terry."

And as I departed I was aware, from the Petitot's manner, that she was about to address to Miss Mary Butler an oration or admonition on her indiscretions, which that young lady, tossing back the curls from her forehead, and folding her hands on her knees as she sat amid a heap of flowers and bouquets, prepared to receive with an expression of the utmost composure and resignation.

Every day my grandfather called at the Castle to see me, and now and then he rode out with Mary and myself on the ponies, which went full gallop to keep pace with the slowest trot of his hack.   One rainy morning, on putting his head into the school-room, he said—

" Dan will come over to pack up for you to-morrow, Terry.   The picture has arrived, and it is time for you to return to Lough-na-Carra."

" What picture is it your grandfather spoke of,

Terry?" asked Mary Butler. "He spoke as if you were to go home because a picture had arrived there."

"It is mamma's picture. It was injured going to Dublin to be new framed, and I am very fond of it."

"But you never saw your poor mamma, Terry, I think, and how can you be fond of her picture?"

"But I am, though. I like to look at her. Oh! she is so beautiful! Poor mamma was lost at sea, you know, when I was a baby, and papa died in the army in India just before."

"They were talking about it downstairs one evening, when I was called in with the dessert," said Mary, musingly; "yes, I remember—Major Turnbull was praising your father, and saying what a fine fellow he was; and he said your mamma was the loveliest creature in the world, but——" here she hesitated and looked down.

"But what—oh, Mary! I entreat of you, tell me—what were you going to say? Dear, dear Mary, tell me! You know you cannot say you don't know, for it would not be true."

"Well, Terry, perhaps I have no right to repeat things not intended for me to hear. It might hurt you, too; and it is just as likely Major Turnbull was wrong."

" If you don't tell me, I declare I will ask Major Turnbull this very minute what he said of mamma," I exclaimed, passionately.

" I cannot help that, Terry. But you must say everything that happened when we were talking. I was wrong, perhaps, at first; but I stopped as soon as I could, Terry, for your sake; and I wont say a word more."

I knew my little friend too well. I threw down my book, and with bursting heart ran downstairs to the billiard-room, whence came the click of the balls, and the voices of the party at the Castle, detained indoors by the rain. For a moment I stopped at the door irresolute; in another I stood in the room, astonished at my boldness, and said— " If you please, Major Turnbull, I should like to speak to you for a moment."

The Major was a tall, lean man, with a face almost the colour of an orange, at least as much of it as could be seen between the close frizzled whiskers, which, beginning in two walls above his ears, where they seemed inclined to run into his shaggy eyebrows, grew together, passing two oases of wrinkled cheek, and a thin, high nose, and reinforced in their course by a heavy drooping moustache, grew into a massive beard, black as his short-cropped hair. His eye was keen, dark, and quick, and there was something in his manner which made one feel that it was only by an exercise of self-control, and a desire to be civil, that Major Turnbull was prevented from "ordering" one whenever he spoke. He had a cue in one hand when I entered, and was patting the other with the upper part, as he surveyed the table and meditated a stroke. "Hullo!" quoth the Major, turning round, and putting his cue butt on the ground, as with his left hand he removed a cigar from his lips and let out a prodigious cloud of smoke. "And what the deuce do you want with me, my little man?"

"Please, Major, I want to speak to you alone, if you please."

"I say, Turnbull, this looks serious. Shall I finish your game for you?" cried Mr. Casey. "It is a cartel Terry has brought you, depend on it; I never saw so grave a youngster in my life."

"What is it, my boy?" quoth the Major, kindly. "Speak out, and tell me what it is you want of me."

"Indeed, Major Turnbull, I want to speak to you quite alone—only you and I two together." I looked at him alone, and saw the quaint look in his eyes.

" What on earth can it be ? However, I never refuse an interview to a gentleman, and we will have it out," he said, with a smile, " as soon as I have finished this game of billiards. Sit down there beside Lady Hautonby till it is over, Terry."

" No, Major," I replied, for I was so impatient and angry I could scarce keep in my tears of vexation ; " I will wait for you outside in the hall, if you please." And as I withdrew I heard a laugh, and Lady Hautonby exclaimed—" What a rude ungallant boy. I shall not forgive you, Major Turnbull, for exposing me to such a rebuff."

But I did not care. The click clack of the balls, the pauses between, the drawling call of the gentleman who was marking—" Fawty-taw ! Thawty-noine" — grated on my ear, and seemed interminable ; at length there was a thumping of cues on the floor, and a clapping of hands, and then Major Turnbull, who had won the game, came out in the best humour in the world, and said—" Well, my little man, and what do you want to see me for ?"

" Do come into the greenhouse, or into the corridor, or anywhere that I can speak to you," entreated I. " Oh ! you can't think how miserable I am."

" Whew !" whistled the Major. " By Jove, this is the oddest thing. Just fancy! Here am I going along led by the sleeve to be made a confidant of by this Tartar of a boy. Eh? miserable, Terry? why then you must be in love—or maybe you owe money in Kilmoyle, to Mrs. McNulty, for gingerbread. One can be cured; the other, especially at your age, is beyond me." I did not mind his talk, but led him unresisting by the arm till we came to a glass-covered passage leading to the greenhouses. No one was there. I shut the door, and then stopping in front of the Major, who was now regarding me with an expression of wonder, and a certain air of alarm, I said—" Major Turnbull, did you ever see my mother?"

" Eh, what?—your mother?—Mary Billing? 'Billing and Cooing,' as we called her. Egad, I should think so—often and often; why do you ask, Terry?"

There was something in his tone which hurt me. " I know she is dead, and I never can see her, Major Turnbull. Oh! if you knew how I love her. I can only look at her picture. I can never find out all I want to know about her. No one will talk of her. But you have seen her, and you knew her, Miss Butler has heard you speaking of her. Oh, do, Major, tell me all about her, and I will pray for you on my knees night and morning."

The Major was moved. He flopped down on one of the seats, and said kindly—" Come here, Terry; sit beside me and tell me what you want to know. It's odd," he said, musingly, " it is very—very odd. Here, now, is her picture driving her poor little son as mad as——well, no matter." He went on after a pause—" Your mother, Terry, was, without exception, the loveliest creature I ever saw. She was at once pretty and beautiful. That picture, though it's good enough, is no more equal to her than that," said the Major, snapping his fingers for want of a better simile. " Lovely ! by Jove, I should think so. Ask Towser, who literally went mad about her !   Ask Jack Nicholson, who went to the dogs about her !   Ask——but what the deuce am I talking to you about ?   I tell you, my dear Terry, every man Jack of us, when I was quartered, years ago, at Cawnpore, was perfectly raving about her beauty, and her grace, and her fascinations, and her accomplishments.   No, I'm wrong there—hold hard—Belle Billing was not accomplished.   In fact, how could she be !   She never was in Europe, and they don't do the finishing touches in India— in fact, can't educate anything but natives, tigers, bad livers, and the pagoda-tree. Besides, old Billing was an awful scamp. That is——You see, Terry, being your grandfather, I should not say that, perhaps—but he *was* a terrible fellow for beer and play. No doubt about it. Ask any old Indian when you grow up what Beery Billing was. He was not in the Company's service — not regularly. He had been brought up under old Skinner. He was rather a pet of Sadut Ali—he commanded the crack regiment of the King of Oude, and, by Jove, usedn't he to give it to the talookdars. I remember hearing——"

"Oh, dear Major Turnbull," interrupted I, "tell me about him after. Now let me hear you speak of poor dear mamma."

"Poor dear mamma!" said the Major, repeating my words twice, and emitting another cloud of tobacco. "Do you know that sounds very funny? Fancy this great Irish lad talking to me here in the middle of Ireland of Molly Billing as 'poor dear mamma!' Egad, it is astonishing. Yes—let me think—Well, as I was saying, your mother's father married some girl who came out on spec with a cargo of spins—a Miss Deighton, I remember it was, because poor Jem Deighton, who was some sort of relative of hers, had a quarrel with Billing about his treatment of her, and hit him through the shoulder, which made Billing behave worse to her than ever. She went off—That is—hem—there was a separation, you know. Your grandmother died soon after, and old Billing was left with one little daughter, who was brought up quite among the natives. That was your mother. She could talk Persian like an interpreter, and understood all the dialects, and played on their cursed instruments.—Aye, by Jove, she made music out of them, too, though it's almost incredible. I'm not quite sure if she didn't wear bangles when she was young, and I know she had a tiny hole in her nostril, where they made her wear a ring till she took it out. Well, Colonel Billing got into trouble with the Oude people at last. He burned a fort with a talookdar in it, by way of making him pay up his taxes, and it was said he didn't keep his accounts on the square. He fled to Cawnpore with his daughter, then a little creature, the loveliest you ever saw, and lived at the various messes, pestering the Government, when he was sober, with petitions and memorials, and plotting with rascally malcontents in Lucknow, and going from bad to worse—in fact, he was a tremendous scamp. I'm sorry to say so of your grandfather, Terry. Driving home one night from mess, old Jack Billing insisted on putting his buggy over a cliff near the river, and saved some one the trouble of breaking his neck. The Belle was sorrier for him than he deserved. As I tell you, his daughter grew up more beautiful every day. All the ladies of the station were delighted to have her with them till she became the belle, and then she had a bad time of it with the young ones. They said she was flighty, extravagant, mischievous—all sorts of things. But no one could stand her smile and her playfulness when she desired to gain them. The Brigadier's wife was like a mother to her, and it was believed they would adopt her. Your father's regiment came to the station just after her father's death. In less than two months we were all envying poor Brady—one of the dearest, kindest, bravest, simplest souls ever God put breath into— for his good fortune in being about to marry the Belle of India. That is, the young fellows did. Some of the old 'uns, and all the women, shook their heads. 'I hope they may be happy,' said the Brigadier's wife to me—I was a sub then, and aide to the general—'but I fear it may not be so.' It was in the evening, as we were looking at the last of the litters moving off to the hills where the bride and bridegroom were going to spend

their honeymoon. I was rather startled, for Mrs.
Crosby was a kind, good woman, and hated scandal,
and was as fond as a mother of Mary Billing. 'Can
there be any doubt of it, my dear madam?' I exclaimed. 'I can answer for him with my life; and
you know what she is.' 'Alas! I do not,' said Mrs.
Crosby. 'I confess I never could understand her.
She could win any one in a moment; but when she
had won him or her, she flung away her triumph and
cared for it no longer. I almost fancy, if a human
creature could be so, she has no soul—like that water-
maiden of De la Mothe Fouqué. She is so vain, so
fond of pleasure, so intensely selfish. Poor thing,
she is very young; and then think how she has
been brought up. I almost fancy she loved Charles
Fraser at one time. After the race ball I spoke to
her about him. She reddened a little, and said—
'Oh, yes; Charlie is a dear daddy long-legs. But
he's got no rupees, and so, my dear Mrs. Crosby,
I have told him it is no go.' 'Well, but,' said I,
'Captain Brady is not over troubled with rupees
either.' 'No; but then she had heard he had
a rich old father, and a fine place at home, and
that he had noble relations, great prospects, and was
certain to get on in the army.' 'He has no noble
relations in England,' I remarked. 'There is a

Spanish grandee of the name who is related to them. He has a cousin a field-marshal of the empire and a count; and another who is head chamberlain to the King of Naples.' She laughed and said—"It's all the same to me. What do I care about England? I was never there. His burra sahibs in Spain and those other places will like me all the better." The fact is, dear Mr. Turnbull, she is, I am sorry to say, rather ignorant, and very selfish. I was pained to see her face yesterday when I took out my jewel-case to give her some presents. You saw the diamond and emerald set she wore? Well, it was in the case in which I have my court diamonds, which belonged to my aunt, Lady Trafford, and when I gave them to her, her eyes were fixed with a look which made me feel almost cold on the large diamonds, and she seemed quite disappointed when I closed the box.' I'm telling you"—the Major had gone on smoking and talking, and now stopped—"Terry, what Mrs. Crosby said. Don't cry, my lad, I did not say I believed it."

"Yes," I sobbed, "you are all abusing her—all down on my poor dead mother."

"Terry," said the Major, gravely, "if you go on in this way I will tell you no more; and, begad, I think I have told you a good deal too much."

I pressed his hand, and my eyes entreated him to forgive me.

"Well, but what use will it be?" remonstrated the Major. "You ask me to tell you all I know, and you get fretted if I do. I was only telling you what a very good kind friend of your mother's said of her before her marriage. In fact, I know little more, my lad," he continued, slowly, "than that your father and mother came back from the hills, where they had been very gay and hospitable, giving splendid parties, which he detested; and they lived very fast in the plains—a large establishment. I am obliged to talk to you as if you understood all these things, you see. I dare say your grandfather can tell you it cost a lot of money. Any way the thing could not go on without a great fortune to back it. But any one who could have seen the—ah, yes, Mrs. Brady—in all her glory, driving her little pony team to the band parade, with no end of mounted grooms and chuprassies, and running footmen in attendance, beheld the gay *levée* round her carriage, and watched her receiving homage from every man jack within miles of the station, would have thought ruin a cheap price to be the husband of such a brilliant being as Mem Sahib Brady Mohtee. I can tell you, as I said, but little more. The Brigadier's time was up, and I went back to my regiment soon after their return."

The Major paused for a moment. He reflected and continued—"You know, Terry, your father had a bad wound before his marriage? Well, he got very weak and ill. He was ordered home on sick leave; but it sometimes happens that a fellow can't go when the doctors bid him. I heard of his death, poor dear fellow, when I was up bear-shooting in Kashmir, after you were born. And the next thing I heard was the loss of the *Ross-shire*—the wreck in which you were saved, and so many were lost, my poor boy!"

"Yes," I cried; "I was saved! Why was I not lost with my darling mother? I am quite miserable when I think of it. Grandfather is very kind, but I would sooner have been washed away with her than live on always thinking—thinking—dreaming, and wishing to see her—Oh! so sick I am wishing —and all in vain."

"This, boy, is quite absurd. Why, if your

mother"—the Major broke out, dashing down his cigar—" could, by cutting off a curl of her hair, save—well—herself. You see she was that kind of woman who isn't easily understood; and, by the Lord, Terry!" he added, "I am not sure this moment what became of her. If she didn't want to be drowned, hang me if the Indian Ocean could do it."

" I cannot understand you. Are you not sure she was lost ?"

" Oh, yes, of course.—But—oh, yes! certainly lost," said the Major, lighting another cigar. " Lost beyond all manner of doubt. You see, Terry, there was awful confusion on board—a crowd of native women, ayahs, and all that sort. Your mamma's name was put in the list of those who perished. I wonder, by the by, what they would have done at Lough-na-Carra had your mother arrived there with all her staff. Do you know, she left Calcutta with seventeen domestics, male and female! Some of the women certainly went over the side—no doubt of that. When I tell you, Terry, that all the questions you have put to me are due to my saying several of the passengers declared they saw your mother at Galle after the ship put in there, you may fancy how wrong I was to repeat such gossip, and get myself into this long confab with you."

" But if she was alive after the wave washed the others away, and the ship arrived at that place, where did she die, or what became of mamma?"

" Pon my honour, Terry, I don't know. When I said ' they,' I should properly have said ' she,' for it was only Mrs. Trimmer, who came with your mother from Lucknow, where she went after her husband's death, that said it."

" And what did she say, sir?"

" Mrs. Trimmer was a chatty old person—much given to scandal, Terry. She used to tell us all at Leamington she was quite sure she saw your mother in Galle, walking to the quay, and that she went off in a boat to a foreign ship which was bound for the French settlement below Madras— Pondicherry it's called."

" Why should she go there if she were safe?"

" That's more than I can say."

" And what became of the servants?"

" They? Oh! they stopped at Galle; all except that precious fellow your native nurse. Captain Fraser, who was on board coming home, and who was taking charge of your mamma, arranged all that, and could have told you more than I can. But he was taken ill at Galle, and when he recovered, instead of coming home he went back to India, and has never returned since. I declare," said the Major, looking at his watch, " it's near lunch time. Now, my dear lad, I've told you everything I think you would care to know; and were you not the son of my dear old friend, I assure you I should have thought you rather a bore. Good-bye; we'll meet often, I dare say."

He was opening the door, when a thought struck him, and closing it, he said softly—

" I am thinking it is very foolish of you to disturb your mind by this anxiety about your mother, who must be dead and gone so many years. It will be better for your peace to think of it no more. Always keep your father's memory in honour, for he was a trump. And remember, Terry, I can't do much, but if ever you want any-thing except advice or money—if I gave you the first it would be bad, perhaps; and of the second I've little indeed—come to me for your father's sake, and I'll do my best. Good-bye, again."

I sat in a state of bewilderment which caused the Major's words to sound as if they came to me in a dream. I had read of miraculous escapes from shipwreck—how a plank or a spar had borne some half-lifeless creature into a calm creek, or a wave had cast him ashore; and how, after years of absence, the lost one had returned to friends and home. I had oftentimes pictured to myself a nook in some lone islet, where, surrounded by strange plants and flowers and animals, tamed by her beauty and gentleness, my mother was living—perhaps with her faithful servant, perhaps held in mild captivity by amiable savages. India was to me a land of marvels and wonders—the haunt of genii and magicians. Why might not the lovely girl have been carried in safety by some subtle charm through the seas, and found a haven in one of the happy isles? "Telemachus," the "Tales of the Genii," "Robinson Crusoe," "Perilous Adventures," and the "Arabian Nights," lent their aid to a hundred devices, conjectures, and theories. I vowed over and over again that the first use of my independence and manhood should be to make full exploration of all the reefs, and caves, and islands far and near, where the cruel sea had played its part. Many I a happy hour had spent in the imaginary search, crowned by the bliss of discovering what I sought for. Into these secrets of my soul I let no one pry; they were kept and nurtured for myself alone; I feared to expose my meditations and my plans to the rough criticism which might destroy the illusions. But now, somehow or other, the story I had just heard seemed to search them out—the ideal I had enshrined in my heart was rudely shaken in its place. " Billing and Cooing, as we called her"—" Belle Billing !"—these and other words he had used about "fellows being in love" with her—the account of her father—the tone in which he spoke, as if she were an extravagant, heartless creature, who had not made my father happy, and who flirted with every one, and was so selfish ! " Could it be true ? No ! Do not believe them, Terry ! Nature itself pleads in your breast against these thoughts. And instead of confirming the story of her fate, the Major's gossiping reports render it all the more likely she is living."

The grating of wheels on the drive outside interrupted my reflections. It was the old carriage from Lough-na-Carra, and I hastened away to my room to get ready for my return.

" And mamma's picture has come home, grandpapa?" I asked, in great glee, as we were driving back. " I shall be so glad to see her again."

" Yes; your favourite study is in its old place. I must tell you that I have decided on sending you

to Dublin to school; and as you are so very fond
of that picture, I have got an artist to take a copy
of it, which you can have and hang up in your
room when you go to Dr. Ball's, next month."

The blow of the announcement was softened, but
the effect of the surprise, the new idea that I was
to leave Lough-na-Carra, prevented my saying a
word.

"Dr. Ball is an excellent man," continued my
grandfather; "he will take every care of you, and
you will not be alone. Maurice Prendergast is
going there too, and you will leave together in a
few weeks. It will only be till Midsummer, when
you come home for the holidays."

Maurice Prendergast was the son of a country
gentleman who had a small estate not very far from
Lough-na-Carra. He was a good-looking boy,
about my own age, but less strongly built; and
Mr. Nolan, who had been entrusted with the charge
of his education, declared he was "*impiger, ira-
cundus, inexorabilis*—a temper rather of Achilles than
of Hector—in fact, a perfect young divil at times,
as the Prendergasts were apt to be." Still it was a
comfort to have him as a companion; and my regrets
at my departure were much diminished when on
running into the old room I saw underneath the

picture of my mother, resting on the floor, a canvas of the same size, with a copy so fairly executed as to give little cause for objection. The eyes were more blue, the colour on the cheeks was brighter, the teeth were whiter, the hair fairer, but the expression was at first sight pretty nearly the same; and it was only on a close examination that I missed something in the copy which was in the original, and yet I could not say what. Under the new frames of the pictures were tablets, on which was inscribed, " Mary, wife of Captain Brady : ætat. 16. Obiit 27th May, ætat. 18."

CHAPTER V.

THE JOURNEY.

It was on a bright frosty morning towards the end of January that the Sligo royal mail drove up to the "Desmond Arms," in the town of Kilmoyle, to change horses, and to take up the two juvenile passengers who had been sitting in the parlour and running out every now and then to take a look up the main street for the coach. Mr. Prendergast and the Doctor were discussing politics, the Reform Bill and the Repeal of the Union, over the fire. Maurice and I, proud of the permission to travel outside, had arranged our luggage in two piles at the door, and were discussing the probable character of Dr. Ball.

"He is an awful fellow for caning, I can tell you. He used to lick my father till he was black and blue: and Dan Casey was taken away because the doctor battered him so," said Maurice. " But that was a long time ago, and he can't be so strong. If he tries to whale me," he added, setting his teeth, "I'll kick his shins and blacken his eyes."

"Whose?" exclaimed I, "Dan Casey's?"

"No," answered Maurice, fiercely, "Dr. Ball's, or any one else's who ventures to beat me."

"But if you deserve it?"

"No matter, whether or no. I'll try not to deserve it, and if I can't help it that's not my fault, and I'm not to be licked for what I can't help. But I say, what have you got there?"

The helper had just brought in a large square case and put it up against the wall near my boxes.

"That's my mother's picture," I replied. "It's going to Dublin with me."

"But you're not going to take it to school with you?" said Maurice. "You'll have all the chaps laughing at you."

"I am, indeed; let them laugh, and welcome. Here comes our coach."

The four horses, with outstretched necks, dilated nostrils, and heaving sides, were already going off to the stables, wreathed in steam, and Mr. Tunks, the coachman, was surveying us over the rim of a glass of "spirits," his red face rising from a cloud of

mufflers, and his drab coat of many capes just leaving a glimpse of the scarlet and gold lace which were
the admiration of the road in fine weather; the
only sign of his dignity as a royal servant now
visible being a broad gold band on his battered
wide-brimmed beaver; as my grandfather and Mr.
Prendergast emerged from the inn in conference
with M'Cluskey, the Guard—a short, square-set,
active fellow, with a quick brown eye, high check
bones, and broad face. "I'll never lose sight of
them till I hand them over to the doctor's man
at the post-office. The two outsides that were
booked from Boyle, Mr. Tunks," he added to
the coachman. Mr. Tunks gave a grunt. It
was his usual style of conversation, and it was
quite wonderful how much he could make the
guttural sound express. There was a tradition
that many years ago he was a colloquial, lively
sort of person, but that having overturned his
coach and killed a passenger by careless driving
whilst conversing with the box-seat, he had
made a vow against gratuitous speech, and had
kept it.

"Now thin, Pat, look sharp there. Get up
these things, you and Owney. And what's that?" he
shouted, as the two men took up my wooden case,

" what in the name of all that's good are you going to do with that ?"

" It's Lough-na-Carra luggage, Mr. M'Cluskey, belonging to the young masther."

" And, shure, don't you see it can't go? It can't go into the box, anyway, and I can't have it stuck up there, as if it was a dining-table at Dublin Castle."

" Well, never mind, Terry," said my grandfather, " it shall go up by the coach. It will be only a day after; this is the mail, and they don't take such heavy things. Now mount, my boy; you have the two seats behind the coachman."

The doctor embraced me affectionately, old Mr. Prendergast shook hands with his son, Mr. Tunks clambered up to his perch, exhibiting two enormous top boots in the feat. The Guard had sprung lightly into his seat, and the helpers were just about letting go the horses' heads, whilst Mr. Tunks's whip-lash was describing a long curve in the air, when there was a cry of " Stop ! stop a minute !" and a groom in the blue and white livery of the Castle dashed alongside on a smoking horse, with a parcel under his arm, and a little note, " it's for you, Masther Terry. The young missus sent it to you, and Sir Richard's put something inside.

Begorra, the mail was nigh startin' too soon for me." In another instant, to the "All right behind!" of the guard, the leaders were let go, the Guard executed a flourishing and broken version of "Garryowen" on his Kent bugle, and amid "God bless you!" from the dear grandfather, and the "hurroo" of the crowd of idlers always present on such occasions, the Sligo mail went off at its fixed rate of nine Irish miles an hour.

The parcel lay at my feet. The letter, with a large seal, was one of the kind known to young ladies in the pre-envelope period, being a pentagon of many folds, and was directed in a large angular hand to "Master Brady, passenger to Dublin." I opened it, and inside was a piece of paper, rather dirty and discoloured, which proved on subsequent examination to be an Irish bank-note. I read :—

"January 27, Wen'sday Night.

"My dear Terry,—Uncle and mam'selle have let me write to you, and so I write to say how sorry I am you are going to leave us. Mam'selle says I should say this in French; but I think you would like English better. Be sure not to forget us, and say your prayers always. I send you a cake we had made for you; I hope you will like it. Uncle is sorry too you are going.   He hopes you will accept the present he sends you, and that it may be useful. You are not to get into fights; but Major Turn-bull says if any boy tries to bully you you must not let him, and that may lead to fighting.   The cake is a seedcake.   Adieu.

   "Believe me to remain very truly,

      "MARY BUTLER.

"Mrs. Burgess, Mam'selle, and all of us send their regards.

"N.B.—We will see you at Midsummer."

I read the letter twice, folded it up, and put it into the pocket of my jacket, under my greatcoat. When I looked up Maurice was regarding me from under his dark eyebrows with a curious expression, but he said nothing.   I was delighted with the buoyancy of the motion, the rush of the keen air, the wide view across the flat country, bounded by the blue hills over the course of the Shannon.   I had left my *pays de connaissance*—all was new to me.   From time to time Mr. M'Cluskey shouted out scraps of information over the pile of luggage.

"That's Mr. Joyce's, of Beaupark !—there, ever so far beyant, is Persse of Blackcastle !   Look at the Round Tower there—built be the Danes it was,

though the Doctor will have it was Christians had a
hand in it.   This is Ballyduff we're coming into—
divil such a place for pigs in Ireland—and there's
no keeping free of them."

A solo on the horn gave warning to the pigs and
their proprietors of the coming danger, and we
drove through Ballyduff without any serious
casualty, although there was a considerable deal of
grunting from Mr. Tunks, and of grunting and
squealing from the pigs, as they were coerced by
whip and stick to leave their pleasant places.   We
had left the town when Maurice, who had been
sitting silent, said—

" Do you often go to the Castle ?"

" Now and then.   Do you ?   I never met you
there."

" No; we don't visit there much. Papa and
Sir Richard don't agree.   They've had law-suits,
and they have disputes about politics.   Do you
know all the land the Desmonds own was once
ours ?"

" No ! was it indeed, Maurice ?   How did it
become theirs ?"

" Yes.   And all the Lough-na-Carra land, and as
far as you can see from Kilmoyle to the hills near
the sea.   Papa has it all on a map."

"But you haven't told me how it was lost. I thought the Bradys always owned Lough-na-Carra, and ever so much beside."

"That may be; but I tell you what papa says, and though he is poor no one ever dared to say he told a lie. My ancestor came over with Strongbow, and he got ever so much of the west of Ireland—but it has all been stolen from us."

"But then, Maurice, you know your ancestor took it from some one else—some poor Irish chiefs—I believe we are Irish; and perhaps you took our land, you know."

"And why not? We fought for it and won it; that's what I say is the best way. But the laws and religion robbed us of our own, and the only way to get it back is to fight for it. Do you know," he exclaimed, angrily, "that we were punished because we took the side of our lawful king and would not change our religion? and we were called 'rebels' and 'papists' by the traitors and the apostates who were lucky."

"Well, but, Maurice, suppose we were always to go on fighting, there would be no peace. If you could get Sir Richard's lands by force, he would try to get them from you by force again."

"Peace!—I want no peace. I want nothing I

can't keep by my own strength. We all—my father says — Butlers, Geraldines, Desmonds, Bourkes, Prendergasts, Cogans, and Laurences, and the rest —won Ireland under Strongbow for ourselves and not for the king; and some of them have contrived to keep their own, and to take that of the others who would not sneak and toady those English. And the English set us fighting, and made laws to crush us, till they've made us all miserable like that fellow there!"

He pointed as he spoke to a peasant who was driving a pig along, and who drew up by the side to let the coach pass. On his head was something like a battered black saucepan without a handle; his coat was composed of an infinity of pieces, which no art could form into a continuous garment, and through the rents were visible a ragged waistcoat, and through the chinks in the vest could be seen a tattered shirt; his nether man, terminating in a pair of bare feet, blue and red, was imperfectly covered by corduroy pantaloons, patched and torn, making an abortive attempt to effect a junction with his footless stockings of worsted. He seemed in the best of good humour, tossed up his stick and caught it with one hand, whilst he took a sharp haul on his pig's tether with the other, and grinned with delight as he received the Guard's salutation.

"Who is that poor man, Mr. M'Cluskey?" I asked, over the luggage.

"Poor! He? Tim Doolan? Faix, he's not poor at all, at all! I'll be bound Tim has a hundred and fifty goulden guineas in a pot somewhere this minnit. He's a warm man for these parts, pays Major Goff twenty-five pounds a year rent, and has as fine land as any in the county. Och! I wish we were all poor like him, I do. And he drivin' home that pig, that's worth maybe fifty shillings at laste, as it stands."

"I daresay, Maurice," I continued, " that man may hate you and me because he thinks we have his land. I don't understand these questions, but I never come to the dining-room but they're all talking of them, and I detest all about it."

"Do you know Miss Butler, at the Castle, Terry?"

"Yes, of course I do; that little letter that came and the parcel were from her, and Sir Richard sent me a pound note."

"I think she is very pretty. They say if Sir Richard's brother, who is out in India, dies, she will own all the estates, and that if some other old

Butler on her father's side dies also she will be a great heiress in her own right."

I do not know how it was, but I did not like talking to Maurice Prendergast of Mary Butler; and as the novelty of the scene wore off, there was a good deal of monotony in the cold drive of twelve hours to the city, which to my imagination was the finest in the world. At each stage M'Cluskey displayed his activity by leaping from his seat over the rail clean to the ground, and at each stage he duly came to the coach-door with a glass of whisky and water for an inside passenger.

" The colonel's colic is very bad to-day, Mr. Tunks," he said, with a wink; "that's the seventh dandy he's had since startin', poor man !"

Later in the day we were aware that the inside passenger was singing in a very cracked voice, and when we halted for dinner I saw a tall, thin old man, with a very red face, closely shaved, balancing himself with great dignity as he got down. He had a very fierce grey eye, rolling in a kind of watery medium, as though it were preserved in spirits.

" Why don't you hold up your horses, sirrah ?" he burst out, angrily; "you're not fit to drive.

I'm hanged if I don't get you dishmiss, to go breaking gentlemen's necks that way !"

Mr. Tunks merely grunted; and the colonel, eyeing him with much severity as he toddled towards the inn door, shook his fist, and, uttering again the words, " I'll get you dishmiss, shure's my name's Finucane !" drew himself bolt upright, and walked as if on a plank in the same direction.

" Ye'd better take no notice of him, me boys !" said the Guard; " the cross dhrop is on him. Och ! an' faith, it's well there's no other inside to-day, or there 'ud be wigs on the green ! He's shot more than one man—the ould scamp !—before the law put the fear of God into these pistol gintlemin. Ye'll have twenty minits for dinner, and make the most of yer time, and take the value of yer money, I'd advise ye."

There was a fire at the end of the dining-room, before which the colonel had taken his position with his hands under the tail of his bottle-green coat with brass buttons; his head erect, set in a high bandana, his eye menacing.

" Shut that door, you boys,—d'ye hear !—shut that door ! Boys oughtn't to be let travel at all. What's yer names ?—who are ye ? Brady ! Any relation of Mick Brady of Punchestown ? Prendergast, eh? Are you a son of Prendergast that was in the Royals? No. So much the better. He was a scut. I'd tell him so if he was here this minute. I would, by —— !" and he thumped the table till the glasses rang, by which he appeared much mollified. He ate like an ogre and drank like a fish; Maurice and I could scarce take our eyes off him. At last he roared—" What are you boys staring at? If I catch you again, by japers I'll teach, you manners, as sure as my name's Finucane."

We were glad to get up on the top of the coach in the dark, as M'Cluskey, after a note on his bugle outside, came in to announce " Time's up, Colonel; come along, young gintlemin."

" Isn't he a dreadful old wretch? And he has shot men, the guard says."

" I wish I were bigger, Terry, and I'd have thrown something at him for his abuse. Wouldn't he have been astonished if I hit him with a plate on the nose?"

The enjoyment of this picture was diminished by the appearance of the Colonel himself at the door, with the landlord holding a light for him, and a helper with a lantern in attendance.

" Steady there !—why don't you hold that light

steady, and be hanged to you! It's before your time, sirrah! Before your time—look at my wash, —Shure's my name's Finucane, I'll dishmiss you!" —and with sundry lurches and catchings of himself up, the terrible dinner-guest made his way to the coach-door, and with an adroit shove from M'Cluskey was deposited inside. After a silent drive, and wrapping ourselves up in our coats, we slept in our seats, fastened with a strap by M'Cluskey. There was a gleam of lights in my eyes, and a hand shook me—

"Here we are in Dublin. Dr. Ball's man is waiting for you."

CHAPTER VI.

THE SCHOOL.

WE forget the tears and terrors through which we have passed, or, remembering, smile at our sufferings, exquisite as they were at the time, when we speak of our schoolboy life. It was with a feeling of something like dismay that I contemplated the expanse of dark brick, lighted by a solitary lamp over the hall window, which was announced by the Doctor's man as the schoolhouse; nor was it diminished when the drawing of bolts and the grating of locks ceased, and a door, partially opened, permitted a fierce face to be seen by the gleam of a candle held high in air, and a gruff voice inquired—

" What kept ye so late, sir ?"

" It's the mail was late, Mr. Cuffe—that's what it was. An' there's a lot of luggidge, too, for such gossoons."

7—2

I had had visions of a hot supper—of blazing fires—of well-lighted rooms on my arrival; and now I stood with my companion, shivering and hungry, by the yawning expanse of an empty grate, in a gaunt hall, provided with four ancient leather-backed chairs, in which ticked a wheezy but loud-toned clock. The man had deposited our impedimenta, and Mr. Cuffe, who had been surveying it in intervals of his close examination of ourselves, having shut and bolted the door, said—

" Now, Brady! now, Prendergast! which is which? Very well; each of you take up his own things, whatever you want for the night, and I'll show you the way to bed. Don't make a noise, though; do you hear ?"

And without waiting a moment Mr. Cuffe's heels, projecting over the ledge of his slippers, began to move rapidly towards a staircase in the distance, and the receding light of his candle told us there was no time to be lost if we did not desire to be left in darkness. Maurice and I seized on a box apiece, and were pattering over the oilcloth, when Mr. Cuffe, turning on the staircase, hissed out—

" Hish, there ! What d'ye mean by all that noise ? Pull off your brogues, you fellows, or you'll have the whole house awake. You must come up the front way."

Maurice and I did as we were told—we were tired, cold, sleepy, and obedient. Again Mr. Cuffe continued his career—one stair—a vault-like landing—a corridor with polished doors, from which the candle-light was reflected on grim portraits against the wall, terminating in black night—a carpeted floor.

"Make no noise here," whispered Mr. Cuffe. "This is the Doctor's shoot."

There was next a carpeted staircase; then another corridor. Mr. Cuffe turned to the left, and at the end halted at a door covered with green baize, which he unlocked, motioning us to pass through, and then locked at the other side. We were in a low whitewashed hall with doors on both sides, and outside each door was a little mound of shoes and boots of all sorts. A sound like the echoes of some distant surf saluted our ears; and Maurice, answering my look of wonder with a nod, said, as we walked along—

"Do you hear them snoring? What a lot of them there must be!"

As Mr. Cuffe proceeded down the passage, he halted now and then and listened at the doors.

and I was aware as we proceeded of creakings behind us as if one were gently opened.

"This," said Mr. Cuffe, "is your room—No. 7. You have the best in the lot. Boyd is away — Putland is in the sick dormitory; and there's only Grierson and——"

Just at this moment some heavy body flying through the air, and skimming over my head, came from behind. In an instant we were in darkness, as Mr. Cuffe, with one hand on the door-handle, was lighting us into our bedroom.

"I'll pay you off for that! I know you, my boy," gasped the tutor, who had been knocked against the door by a hard bolster. "You boys, go in, and wait till I come with the light. Just look out, O'Brien, for that."

As Mr. Cuffe groped his way along the passage, we heard the door at the end open and shut. In a moment there was a pattering of many feet, and a rustling as of a storm in the air. The noise enveloped us. I was caught by the hair just as I heard Maurice shout out—

"I say, none of that! If you hurt me again I'll knock you down."

It was a rash threat, and I suffered for it as well as he. The urchins who were around us knew no mercy, and did know the room; and joined by the two boys who were in it, furious at being roused from their sleep, Maurice and I, striking out blindly, were pinched, cuffed, bolstered, and throttled by unseen arms, till a whistle sounded at the end of the passage, when the pattering, rustling, and thumping sound was renewed, and died out in a creaking of doors, and in a minute more a light and Mr. Cuffe, with a candle in a lantern in one hand, and a cane in the other, appeared.

"Och! och! and so they've been bolstering you, have they! You must put a penny to your eye, Brady. Now, you Grierson—you Cole! don't be shamming there. You'll have to report who did it in the morning to the doctor."

Grierson and Cole were very fast asleep indeed —Cole's snoring was of the most solid and portentous character, indicative of apoplexy; Grierson, who lay in the next crib, had a sweet unconscious expression on his face, which was, however, scarce in character with his puckered-up mouth and shut eye.

"That's your bed, Brady; that's yours, Prendergast. You may lock yourself in to-night. There's your candle. The first bell will ring at half-past six; prayers at seven."

Mr. Cuffe shut the door and retired; and Maurice and I were left to our meditations.

"You'll have a black eye, Terry," said he, "from those blackguards."

"And your mouth is cut, Maurice," returned I. "Let us get to bed, I feel so tired."

As I turned to my box I was aware that Grierson was sitting up in bed, and that Cole had both eyes wide open.

"I say, did I hear you call me a blackguard?" asked Grierson.

"Yes," returned Maurice, fiercely; "you or any one who'd attack two strange fellows in the dark like that for nothing."

"Will you be licked to-morrow, or will you have it now?" asked Master Grierson, with much earnestness, getting out of bed as he spoke, and advancing towards Maurice.

I saw that he was a stout, tall, fair-haired chap, with a flat flabby face, at least an inch taller than Prendergast, and I ran in between them, saying—

"No; you shall not hit him. You are a cur, and if you want to fight you must fight me."

Master Grierson saw, perhaps, I was a little more of his match, though still a year younger, and somewhat lighter than he was.

" You're a cocky cub enough, I daresay. Now
then, Cole, you hide that fellow, and I'll manage
this," and, squaring his arms, he commenced his
preparations for battle. Whilst we were parleying
in elegant prelude, Maurice had gone to the door,
locked it, put the key in his pocket, and coming
alongside me, said—

" Terry, I'll stand by you to the last, and we
will give them a thrashing for the honour of Kilmoyle. Now come on."

His face was dark with passion ; the blood
stealing over his lip gave him a savage look ; and
Cole, who did not quite understand why he should
be called on to break his night's sleep, suggested a
basis for negotiations of peace.

" If you have got anything in your boxes we
will let you off," he said. " Shan't we, Daddy ?"

" Let us see what the louts have first, and if it's
worth taking, we shan't lick them."

And acting in that spirit, Grierson made a rush
at the box which stood beside my bed, and which
I had been uncording when he thought fit to rouse
up. With a spring I stood before him, and
shouted,

" You musn't touch my things ;" and as I said
so, received a blow in the face which sent me

staggering towards the middle of the room. It was but for a second. I knew nothing of boxing, but I was strong and active, and in the twinkling of an eye my knuckles tingled with the sharp, quick jar produced by a blow delivered on a bone,. and blood ran from Grierson's lip.

I cannot tell what followed. I was aware that Cole and Maurice were engaged in a similar struggle; whilst Grierson and I pummeled and cuffed each other, and scuffled and wrestled all over the room.

Chairs were overturned — water-bottles and basins and basin-stands went crashing on the floor. Like most Irish boys, we were unacquainted with any scientific mode of giving black eyes and bloody noses, but eyes were puffing and swelling, and noses and lips were bleeding on both sides.

My antagonist was more used to such encounters; but I had learnt a little of a rude sort of wrestling. I had the advantage, besides, of being dressed, whilst he was in his shirt; so, whenever we closed, I generally managed to throw him. Once his head came with force against the edge of my box, and I gasped out—"Do you give in?" And was answered by a feeble blow in the ribs. Still his strength was failing, and fall after fall brought him nearer to submission; Maurice and Cole, better matched, perhaps, were whirling in the eddies of combat among the beds and overturned chairs.

"Let us in to see fair play." Gentle knocks and urgent entreaties proclaimed the anxiety of the boys, who had been aroused by the scuffle, to join in the fray. But we were little inclined to listen to such appeals! With nostrils distended, fast-closing eyes, dishevelled hair, swollen hands and lips and cheeks, and torn clothes, the only sounds inside the room being our heavy breathing and the thumps of fists, and the knocking about of the scanty furniture, we fought on till a sharp cry escaped from my opponent; and he exclaimed "Oh, my foot! my foot!" He had trodden on a piece of glass. I was terrified. Cole, hastening to his friend, who was sitting on the bed in agony, ran to the door and cried out—

"Some of you ring the doctor's bell; here's Dick Grierson cut his foot open."

I had seen at my grandfather's people brought in with accidents, and in imitation of what I had observed, I poured out water in a basin, tore a strip off one of the shirts in my box, and bathed the cut; but the glass was inside, and I could not staunch the wound.

Maurice had unlocked the door, and was standing beside Cole, watching the fainting boy with terror and pity, when we were aware of a tall man gliding among us; his white hair flowing over his shoulders from the silver band of a large black velvet cap; his face, round and florid and smooth, animated by an expression full of repose and calmness. His figure was shrouded in a dark velvet dressing-gown; and although he had not long been roused, Dr. Ball looked as if he were quite ready to sit for his portrait; his theory, indeed, being, that no one should ever be in such a hurry as not to be able to appear in the utmost propriety of dress. He looked at the scene before him with some kind of curiosity, if not surprise, laid down his candlestick with deliberation, and sitting down on the bed beside Grierson, having previously placed a handkerchief across his own knees, took his leg upon his lap, and examined the cut in silence. Then he put his hand into his breast, drew out a small case, and produced from it a spiteful-looking, shining implement of steel, with which he firmly seized the glass, and by a steady tug, which made the lad utter a bitter cry, pulled it out of the wound. At the doorway were shadowy faces; a faint murmur came from the passage as the doctor, selecting another implement from his case, passed it to and fro in the fissure. Then with lint from the same inexhaustible case, and with water and scissors he made a bandage round the wound, placed the limb on the bed, took up his candle, and surveyed us slowly one after the other.

" Such are the fruits of disobedience—the results of strife and contention," he said at last. " If you were the beasts of the field, you could not tear and wound each other more cruelly; but the beasts have none to guide them—you have. They have none to correct them—you shall find that you have. Mr. Cuffe," he added, " stay in this cubicle to-night in one of the spare beds. The surgeon must see Grierson early in the morn-ing." And the tall figure vanished.

I felt relieved when he went; and yet I wished he had said something to me. There was a cold displeasure in his eye as he looked into my face, more hard to bear than words. It was a keen reproach to be stared at with such haughty contempt; and as I looked at my face in the glass, and turned to Maurice, who had got into bed, and had sullenly given his hand to me, I became aware that our first interview with Dr. Ball was not of a nature to impress him in our favour. My eyes were puffed and painful, and my cheeks shining and swelled out with blows; my lips like a negro's. Maurice was not much better; Cole and Grierson bore similar marks of the fray; and Mr. Cuffe, as he walked round us with his candle, had some reason for saying, "Our mothers would not know us;" though he little understood the significance of his remark in regard to myself.

Dr. Ball began his college career as a Fellow Commoner and an idler; of a fine person and manner, he associated with the wildest set of his year in days when there were really wild young men in Trinity, and ere it had ceased to be a staid training-school sort of place ; and he drank, hunted, and played with the blue bloods of the Irish university, before Oxford and Cambridge came into fashion for Irish students, and such appearances in the world as Swift, Goldsmith, Sterne, and Burke became impossible. It was supposed old Mick Ball, the linen-merchant, would leave his only son all his money. His son acted on the supposition. One day old Mick called in on him in Botany Bay Square, and found the young gentleman sitting at a well-appointed table. It was twelve o'clock, and old Mr. Mick Ball glowered at the silver on the cloth and the decanter

of claret, and the tea things, with a puzzled, dis-
contented look.

"Is it breakfast or dinner yer atin, Dinny?"

"Well, sir, you see it's a sort of composition
between the two—a snack you would call it in the
old time—lunch, let us say. How very well you
are looking, to be sure, this morning."

"Am I, Dinny? I don't feel so. I've been
over to yer chewther's" (Dinny's face slightly moved),
"and what he tells me isn't like to make me feel
pleasant."

"Indeed, sir! Some wars, or rumours of wars.
Apprehensions concerning flax, or combinations in
the political world affecting linen? I hope not."

"No, Dinny; its rhumers about yerself, an' its
combinations affectin' my pocket, that thrubbels
me. Now listin awhile. The divil an honour
ye'v tuk since ye inthered. You ought to be a
scholar this year, yer chewther tells me. There's
young Brophy, of Skinner's Alley, got one, an' is
always gettin' honours, and he'll be a Fellow, an'
maybe a bishop before he sthops. It's nearer pluckin'
you get every time, and fine feathers they'd get off
you. Here have I been slavin' an' toilin' an' moilin'
early and late up in the office, an' goin' about
thinkin' of nothin' but webs and yarns and flax, that

you might turn out a credit to me an' to the poor mother that's dead an' gone. I've been proud of seein' you wid the bucks, tho' you and young Thrimblestone nigh rode over me last week as I was crossing Grafton Street, widout by yer leave, in yer red coats. I've paid all your debts, and given you a fine allowance—an' yer had the best of cattle to ride ; an' all I asked in return was that you'd just get an honour, and do something for the family, like young Plunkett, and lots of others. An' Mr. Nagle says you're as clever as any of them, wid a good head for mathematics and larnin' of all kinds. An' what have you done? Answer me that ! I'll tell you. Ye'v been givin' the supper parties that's breakin' the hearts of the Dane and Faculty. Ye'v been neglectin' the lecthers and chapels. Ye'v been out wherever there's the sportin' an' gamblin' goin' on; keepin' dreadful hours. Ye'v been givin' post obits, an' things of that kind, speculatin' on yer father's death. Yer deep in debt to all the money linders in Eustace Street. An' what am I come for now ?—to ask you to sthop in time, an' behave well to me, an' I'll behave well to you."

"My dear father, believe me——"

"No ; I'll believe nothin' but deeds. Go on as

you like—do as you like—but a return for my money out of you I expect, or you'll be disappointed when I'm gone, Dinny. To show you I'm in earnest I've brought you these."

The old man produced a pocket-book of many pockets from an old case.

"There's yer acceptance to Mulloy for £200—paid; there's yer account with Hennessy, for horses, £427 16s.—paid; there's French's account, £180—paid; there's another of Mulloy's—there's one of Tuke's — here's O'Neale's—there's Dempsey's — a nice lot, 'pon me word—to the valley of £903 paid—that's gettin' on to two thousand pounds, Dinny; And here's an order on Latouche for £300 for debts I want to know nothing of. I start you fair, I hope? And now no speeches. Burn those blaggard papers. Ye'v three months to the next examination, and I expect to hear of you thin. Good-bye. God bless you. Go on and finish yer — breakfast, Dinny. And remimber—ye can't ate yer cake and have it."

The old man kept his word. On a certain morning in the month of July the Dublin papers contained an advertisement:

"NOTICE.——I hereby give notice that I will not be responsible for the debts contracted by my son,

Dionysius Ball, Undergraduate, Trinity College, the said Dionysius being of full age.—(Signed), M. BALL, Linen Hall, Dublin."

Another notice announced that " M. Ball, linen manufacturer, having retired from business, had made over the whole of his interest in the Bally-vogue and Ballymena mills and factories, and in the stores in Belfast and Dublin, to his nephew, James Grabb, for whom he requested the support of his old connexion."

When Mr. Dionysius Ball had arrived near the end of his college course his father died.   His will was opened, and it was found that, having paid to his son, and on his account, the sum of £11,703 10s. 6d., he, Michael Ball, bequeathed to him the sum of £3966 9s. 6d., to complete his education in college, and left the rest of his estate to his wife's relations.

Dionysius Ball set to work ; but it was too late. One day a feeble man, nearly blind from study, was led in, with a shade over his eyes, to the Hall in which the Fellowship Examinations are held, and more than usual interest was evinced, as it became known that " Dandy Ball was going in for a Fellowship." There were five competitors for the golden prize.   Dandy Ball was second.

Again and again he tried; always some more
brilliant scholar or riper student stood just above
him.   The examiners, touched by his perseverance,
would have gladly seen him win, but it was not to
be.   After four great efforts he resigned himself to his fate, and became a " grinder," and even-
tually a schoolmaster, having taken out his degree in
laws. He was distinguished for a melancholy gravity,
stately manners, and elegance of dress which
seemed out of place in a Dublin dominie.   His
sole pleasure was found, strangely enough, in assiduous devotion to his pupils, in the study of
mathematical problems, and in preparing editions
of the classics, more remarkable for fine type, paper,
and binding, than for great learning or inge-
nuity.   He had a small living, and refreshed himself
on Sunday by preaching highly ornate and polished
sermons, which principally dealt with the theories
of heathen philosophers, and showed their general
inferiority to the Christian scheme in their relations
to life on earth.

" An' so you've been fightin' already, and have
bet Grierson and Cole secundus," said Larry, as
he brought in our shoes, and roused us in the
morning.   " Faix, purty black eyes as ever I've
seed at Donnybrook !   It's a nate beginnin' you've

med, Prendergast and Brady. Hurry on, and dhress. Dr. Ball wants to see you afore prayers, and thin you've to sthay up here till yer eyes goes out of mourning. Mister Grierson, I'm to have you remov'd to the Sick Ward, and Cole's to shift to No. 8 crib, next dure."

"It is a bad beginning indeed, Maurice," I muttered, as we stood, afraid to knock, outside the door to which we had been shown. "Do you think he'll flog us?"

"Not if he's just. The two big bullies above should get it if any one. I don't intend to be touched, I can tell you." As we spoke, the door was opened from the inside, and the Doctor stood before us; the black velvet cap still on his head, for in my day trencher caps were never used out of college, and a sort of black silk cassock, with upright collar, fitting very tight, fastened round the waist by a band, and coming down so low as only to show the buckles of his shoes, gave him the air of some mediæval ecclesiastic—and the similitude was increased by the flowing white hair, and the snowy turned-over collar and cuffs, which contrasted with his sombre dress.

"Come in, Terence Brady and Maurice Prendergast." We stood in the Sanctum and the Inferno—

at once the place of rewards and of punishments—the Doctor's study : a wilderness of books—the neatness of his person was by no means indicative of habits of order—with books on shelves, books on chairs, on tables, on the carpet, on the chimney-piece. He drew up with his back to the fire, one hand on his hip, the other outstretched, with the finger pointed to me. " Now, Terence Brady, as you are the elder, give me an account of the manner in which the proceedings of last night began. I will not say it is your interest to tell the truth, for I would not appeal to a base motive when you stand in my presence." I told him the truth. As I spoke, he listened attentively, and turned his eyes from me to Maurice, and never asked a question till the close, and then he said— " Brady, do you forgive the boy who began this trouble freely and fully from your heart ?"

" I do, sir."

" Prendergast, I ask you the same question ?"

Maurice hesitated. He looked down and was silent.

" It is not necessary for you to answer me. I regret you still feel enmity to Cole; depend on it you would be happier if you could say as your friend has done. You may go."

If any dreamer cherishes visions of Utopia as

possible realities, let him remember what his life was at a school, and cease to hope. Who can withstand the tyranny of that oligarchy which arises in the little republic, and which has ever a despot of its own? For two years my life was as bearable, in virtue of my prowess on the night of my arrival, as the duresse of attendance and compulsory learning could make it. I was chosen into the upper twenty for our hurling matches after one or two hard fights. Daddy Grierson, the very first day he came into the green where we played, pale and limping as he was, shook hands with me *coram publico*, and declared—" Brady is one of the old stock. The Doctor told me he took all the blame on himself." My reputation was made by the stories which had gone abroad over the school, for Grierson was one of the Ajaxes of the field. Maurice Prendergast did not fare so well. He had refused to make it up with Cole, and the result was a pitched battle, in which Maurice got rather the worst of it, and he was unfortunate enough to appear as if he did not accept the public judgment with good grace. Dr. Ball heard of the encounter, and in ordering him and his antagonist punishment, publicly expressed his regret that one of his boys exhibited such vindictiveness.

Maurice had in him some unhappy knack of thinking everything which occurred in the world of an unpleasant nature was specially ordered with reference to himself — that all around were plotting to do him mischief—that he alone was singled out for annoyance, and perchance for punishment. His spirit was dark and moody. He had listened at home to old stories about the greatness of the family of Prendergast in the time of Strongbow, till he believed their present poverty was the result of a great conspiracy on the part of King, Lords, and Commons; and he was continually revolving schemes in his head for their restoration to the lordship of barbarously-named regions which had long since merged into baronies and counties. The mind of the boy, in fact, was warped by this one idea—that he was the victim of wrong and injustice; and as he was of a studious turn, and read more than most boys of his years, turning his attention to what may be called the fabulous history of Ireland, and swallowing without hesitation the preparations of the annalists and national historians who doctor facts or invent nostrums to suit their theories, he became an eager politician.

There were Repealers and Reformers in those days. Dr. Ball's was an eminently Protestant academy, and Maurice Prendergast chose to avow himself a Repealer and a Reformer, and to stand in a minority of one. You know what the toleration of a school is. It is there that the philosopher may study the way in which the will of a majority, without checks, becomes a cruel despotism. Maurice clung to his faith, and took a gloomy delight in suffering persecution, which was moral rather than physical. There is no misery so great as to burn with the love of country which is treason —to be possessed with the patriotism of a broken nationality, which is sustained by dreams, and visions, and hopes—lives and dies again till the end, whatever that may be — extinction and oblivion—or resurrection. Maurice believed that petitions, and public meetings, and processions of ill-clad citizens, with bad bands and worse banners, would induce the British Government to restore a native legislature to Ireland. He wore a green riband in his cap, and gilt buttons, with a harp and crown, and the device of Repeal, on his coat. He read immense quantities of speeches, and learnt whole Iliads of national poetry, and was looked on as a vulgar malcontent, who must be a rebel at heart, as well as a Papist. He was cut out of our games, and placed under a proscription, which he resented by aggressive war whenever he got a chance. It was with difficulty I could keep on good terms with him because I would not join him in ostracising the whole school; but at night, ere we closed our eyes, we were generally good friends again. I pitied him greatly, for often and often I heard his suppressed sobbing, and his cries in his sleep, and knew how much he endured in his gloomy spirit.

I had my own sorrows. There was for ever, when I was alone, no thought but that one wearing, wearying solicitude that was the morbid centre around which all my future plans were woven. I had a faith that my mother lived. The more I reasoned on the subject, the greater seemed the improbability —the larger and firmer grew the faith. I had of course given up all idea of taking the picture to Dublin the moment I had seen my room and understood the nature of boys at school; but every trait was preserved in my memory, and I made endless efforts to put them on paper, destroying the scraps as fast as I drew them. I grew strong and tall, was famous at hurling, football, and prison-bar, which are the substitutes for cricket. On my half-holidays I went up the little stream which passed the school-gates on its way from the mountains to Dublin Bay. Faithful to my early love, I fished away till night approached, returning, happy, but foot-sore, with my creel pretty well stocked with trout, which the Doctor used to take tithe of for his Sunday morning's breakfast ere he proceeded to his church, a quarter of an hour in advance of the column led by Mr. Cuffe, and closed by the rear-guard under Monsieur Lebœuf. Sometimes Maurice came with me; but he was so immersed in his ridiculous books that he was not much of a companion. Besides, he was always fancying that the boys he met intended to affront him, and was getting into endless rows, in which black eyes and bloody noses were ingredients; and if he took to fishing, it was in a passionate spirit, quite unsuited to the contemplative man's recreation. If the fish were rising, he was in the greatest spirits. The little ones went flourishing in the air over his head, coming down far behind him on the stones with a whack which left them hardly time to shiver ere they died : the big ones, not numerous, carried away gut or flies, or broke tops, or lost their snouts—rarely were they landed; and when Maurice executed a feat of this kind he hopped and jumped about with rage. When an cast wind, or a general indigestion, or some mysterious agency only known to fishes, kept them with their heads below the surface, Maurice, after a few impatient casts—well thrown and fine for the matter of that—would put up his rod in dudgeon, swear there was no use in trying any more, and be greatly surprised when he found my creel pretty full at night. So I was often left alone in my excursions into the mountain valley, where the little stream became a succession of pools of dark peat-coloured water, swarming with tiny hungry trout. Latterly I often met a broad, stout man, of some thirty or five-and-thirty years of age, fishing with more perseverance than success. He had a swarthy, sunburnt visage, black whiskers and eyes, shining white teeth, and a pleasant look and smile—so frank and kindly, that at last I ventured to fish in the pools below him, and to take the liberty of crossing behind and going above him when I saw he took no notice. And then we got on nodding terms.

I was quite glad to hear his cheery voice, although it was only—" Hullo! youngster; and so here you are again. We wont leave a trout in the river between us, though I know who'll take most of them."

And his laugh was delightful as he compared his basket with mine after a while. "Well done, youngster! Two dozen and three. And a couple of whoppers! Just see what I've done—only seven. But I'm getting on—I'm getting on, and I'll beat you at last."

I showed him my flies, and told him what I thought hindered him from being a great angler: he would persist in standing close to the banks, and hopping about from stone to stone, like an ouzel. His delight was great when one day he succeeded in hooking and killing a two-pounder at the tail of a dam. "Dash my wig! but you are right. I've been trying for that fellow ever since I began at this work, and only for you I'd never have caught him. Isn't he a beauty? Talk of dolphins—stuff! There's colour for you—there's speckled sides. I wouldn't take ten gold mohurs for him this moment."

The word "mohur" struck me at once. I had heard it often from Mohun. "Were you ever in India, sir?" I asked.

"Yes, my lad. That is, I've been cruising about in the Indian Ocean—served on the station some time; but beyond a day or two at Madras and at Galle, a sail up the Hooghly, and a short time at Calcutta, I can't say I know much of the land."

" Did you ever know Captain Brady out there, sir ?"

" Brady ! Brady ! What was he, a soldier or a sailor ?"

" Oh, sir, my father was a gentleman: Captain Brady, of the King's Own Regiment," said I, offended at the idea of its being supposed he was a sailor.

" Faith, I beg your pardon ; I forgot our profession is not thought much of in these parts. And so your name's Brady, is it ? And you're at school near here, learning your *propria quæ maribus*— ' things proper to the seas,' as I translated it, and got a hiding—eh ? Where is it ?"

" I am at Dr. Ball's, of Hume Grove."

" Are you going to be a soldier, like your father ?"

" I don't know, sir. I should like to be a soldier, but my grandfather will not hear of it."

" Grandfather wont hear of it ? Rich old codger— must have his way. And what does your governor say of it, eh ?"

" My father is dead ; he died in India several years ago, when I was but a baby."

" And of course mamma sides with grandpapa—does she ?"

" I cannot say, sir. I have not seen my mother. It is supposed she is dead ; but I don't think so."

We had been walking along as we talked ; but as I uttered these words my interlocutor turned round briskly, with a look of surprise on his honest brown face. " Say that again, till I just get its bearings. You haven't seen your mother, and it is supposed she is dead, but you don't think so ! That's a rum sort of thing to say, my lad."

" Well, it is true, sir. They all believe mamma was drowned coming home from India ; but I feel—I feel it here," I said, laying my hand on my heart—" that I shall see her, and that she is alive."

" Dash my wig, Master Brady, but you are puzzling me. And so," he added, with a look of softness in his big round eyes, " you don't like to believe your mother is down among—hem—I mean is drowned ? Why so, if everyone else says she was ?"

" Because no one can be sure of it. When the ship struck she was washed off with ever so many others, and they say she was lost. But the ship was near an island—near Les Basses rocks, off the coast of Ceylon."

" And the ship's name was ?"

" The *Ross-shire* Indiaman."

The angler struck the butt of his rod against the ground and whistled out a prolonged whew-w-w, and repeated my words—" The *Ross-shire!* The Basses ! Why, to be sure ! to be sure ! I remember it well. I was lying in Galle at the time in the *Calypso,* on my first long cruise, and saw her come in after she was got off by the skipper. They made a jolly fuss about his getting her off. He ought to have been reprimanded for getting her on, say I. And Mrs. Brady—the beautiful Mrs. Brady— was your mother, my poor lad? How very, very odd to meet you here !"

My heart was beating so that I could hear it like the wheel of the mill close at hand. " Oh dear, dear sir, did you ever see my mamma ?"

" No," he answered, shortly, " never—often heard of her. But if that Brady was your father I remember him well when he was a sub. at Malta and I was a middy ; and a better fellow never lived—for a soldier, no better. I heard of his marriage, of his death, and of his wife's being drowned from the *Ross-shire,* and I remember well hearing that their infant was on board—wretched little beggar—on his way to Ireland. Oh Lord, to think I should meet you this way, on the banks of the Dodder, in this confounded country." He looked at me so kindly, I took his hand and pressed it, and the honest fellow returned the pressure with a gripe of irresistible vigour. "Here," cried he, "sit down on this bank, and let us talk about everything. It is so very odd to think how things come about. I wish I could recollect all I heard about Brady and his wife. There were lots of stories; but that's of no consequence. The strange thing is you should persist in it that she's alive, my boy; as if it would be any advantage to you if she were, by all accounts. My belief is that she's just as dead—as dead," he said, taking up a pebble and throwing it into the pool at our feet, "as that stone."

I said nothing, but sat looking into the bright stream.

"I tell you what, my lad," he continued, "you go moping about by yourself too much. I'll ask your master to let me give you a cruise now and then in the Bay. Wouldn't that be jolly! My name is Window; any fellow can see through me, they say, and I command the *Merlin* cutter for my sins—a revenue cruiser, if you know what that means. Here, take this card to your schoolmaster, and tell him I will call on him to ask leave to take you out now and then—from Saturday till Monday, you see. We have prayers on board on Sundays—capital chaplain; read service myself; and we'll have a run down to Wicklow and back, if you like."

On the card was "Lieutenant John Window, R.N., H.M.C. *Merlin.*" I knew nothing of the sea; I could indeed see the blue waters of the Bay from my bedroom window, and the white sails of the ships as they slid along from one headland to the other. Oftentimes I noted the trails of smoke from the packets and watched the funnels and masts as they came in sight from behind trees and chimneys; but of the sea itself I had a secret, subtle terror. I remembered little of my early voyage. But the impressions of its force, its cruelty, its irresponsible power, its sullen anger and destroying rage, were derived somehow from the very beginning of my existence, and were mingled with a sort of antipathy to a thing which had done me irreparable wrong. However, the love of adventures such as this, and the getting away from school, were very strong inducements to say "yes," and I expressed my thanks to Lieutenant Window, R.N., for his kindness.

"And now," said he, "I must be off. I have to walk across to the coast near Bray, and I don't want to run out my daylight. I will call soon on old Ball and get leave for you. Good-bye, my lad; you had better top your boom and make sail too." And with a smile which showed his white teeth the sailor turned from the stream, putting up his rod as he went, and was soon making his way with light and active step up the hill-side towards the Three Rock mountain. My path lay towards Dublin, in the outskirts of which the school was situated; and as I trudged back my mind was full of questions which were to be put to my new acquaintance at our next meeting.

CHAPTER VII.

THE CRUISE.

I HAD not long to wait. The next week saw the beginning of the short vacation at Easter, and my grandfather had written to say he thought, as the old house was under repair, and the typhus was very bad in the district, I had better stay at Dr. Ball's. "There is no one at the Castle," he added, "and you will have your friend Maurice to keep you company at all events for your week's holiday."

I was in our cubicle, arranging my flies for a grand excursion which was to last two days, and Maurice was packing up hard-boiled eggs, a pot of jam, and other luxuries, when the servant informed me, "The Doctor wants you, Masther Brady." It was rarely we were summoned to the presence, and I scarcely needed the addition, "I think yer goin' off somewhere, and maybe I'd best get ready yer duds, for there's a gintilman on a kyar has come, and they're waiting below."

When I entered the study the pleasant face of the Lieutenant greeted me. But instead of his fishing suit he had on an undress uniform, and a cap with a gold band in his hand, and looked very smart. Dr. Ball and he had been engaged in looking over the large globe, on which the latter was pointing the course of some voyage in distant seas, and the former was in great good humour, for he had had an opportunity of astonishing his visitor by the accuracy of his knowledge.

" So, Brady, you have met a friend of your father's. I am always glad to promote the education of the gentlemen in my establishment by favouring their intercourse with persons who are able to improve their minds and cultivate their intellects—above all with such enlightened travellers as Mr. Window, a member of a glorious profession, to which England owes so much of its greatness"— here the Doctor bowed, and looked as if he had enunciated some striking and novel proposition— " therefore," he continued, with more dignity, " I have yielded to Captain——"

" Only Lieutenant, if you please, Dr. Ball," interrupted Window, with a laugh.

"I do not please, sir—I think you ought to be Captain Window; but I admit the propriety of your objecting to the use of a designation which were yours already had services such as we are discussing been duly recognised. Pardon the remark; I was saying, Brady, that I have yielded to Lieutenant Window's representations, and have permitted you to go from beneath my tutelage, in order that he may take you on a short marine excursion and impart to you some rudimentary instruction in the art of navigation."

"Nay, Doctor, I'm not quite sure I can promise to do much in that way. You see, when I'm on board I've a good deal to do, though I have no company; and fresh air, plain, wholesome food, and a little change, are all I can promise our young friend, though he may study 'Noric' if he likes. We must look pretty sharp," he added, looking at his watch; "the boat is waiting for us at the Pigeon House, and the cutter is inside the Wall lying-to till we come. The tide's running out, and if she has to go outside we may have a long row, and get wet jackets, for there's been a fresh breeze from the southward, and the sea's not quite gone down."

The Doctor waved his hand, and in a few minutes

I was seated on the car beside Lieutenant Window rattling over the road to Ringsend, at the speed which a Dublin jarvey always considers due to an " officer."

There is ever something or other of acid in the cup of our pleasures : mine was flavoured by a drop distilled from Maurice's eyes. As I hurriedly told him of my little voyage, he looked up from his haversack with a face full of mortification, and said, " I thought so. You might have told me of this before. Just as I am ready for the only little days' pleasure I have had since I came to this horrid place, and was going to see what I was longing for, the Round Tower and all, you throw me over. I can go with no one else. There." He took up his bag and dashed it against the wall, bursting into tears as he spoke, whilst the blood-red stains of the cherry cordial and the jam on the surbase proclaimed the ruin he had made.

I set off, wondering whether I was not really a selfish fellow to disappoint Maurice, and full of regrets for the jam and cherry cordial.

" Yes, my lad, there will be a little swell on when we get into the Bay, but the wind is light, and we'll take a run down towards the Arklow Banks, and maybe we'll show you some of your favourite sport on a large scale."

"Are there any whales, sir ?" quoth I, eagerly. "There are British whales, I know, and I don't see why they should not come to Ireland, too."

"Whales ? No, my lad ; at least, not to catch. If British whales were wise, they'd keep away from these waters ; but there are more sharks than I like—smugglers, in fact. There is a confounded schooner we have heard of, which has run a whole cargo of Yankee tobacco and French brandy lately, between Arklow and this. Stubbs, who had the cutter before me, was removed for that same, and I'm put here to prevent the same occurring again. Hope I may, but can't be sure."

The car rattled along the South Wall, drove slowly over the Pigeon-house Fort bridge, and I was aroused from my survey of what seemed to me the bustling river, filled with craft running down with the tide for sea, by a—" Look sharp, my lad ! here we are. Take these traps, Robert, and stow them away in the gig." Led by Lieutenant Window down the slippery causeway, I took my place where I was told, in. the stern of the boat, which was a marvel of whiteness and brightness in wood, and paint, and brass, in my eyes. The crew, with their clean shirts and snowy trowsers, were in keeping with the boat. As the Lieutenant said —"Now, give way there!" there was a tone in his voice I had never heard before, not near so pleasant and so soft. "There, Brady—or, if you'll let me, Terry—there's the *Merlin*. How do you like her?"

Alas! how full life is of disappointment. I had had more than my share that week. Of all created things, it appeared to me the elephant and the lion must be the grandest: the size and sagacity of the first, the port and courage of the latter, excited my admiration. I had pored over the "Wild Sports of the West," and travels, and natural history, and had formed ideals in my mind, with the help of plates and illustrations, which turned out to be pure illusions the moment I paid my sixpence and entered Wombwell's travelling menagerie. That scrubby, wrinkled, shapeless beast, without any tusks, and with a flabby proboscis, not much taller than our bull "Rogueen!"—that lank-sided, overgrown cat, with a ragged felt of hair over his shoulders, crouching at the sight of the keeper's iron rod!—that an elephant!—that a tiger!—these were bitter things to see and bear! And now there came

another shock.   My grandfather had once made
a voyage on board a transport, forming one
of a fleet under a small convoy which was at-
tacked by the French off Ushant.   I had often
listened to his account of the action, in which not
only the men-of-war but the transports behaved so
well, that they beat off the enemy, and took
Le Grand Condé, of seventy-two guns.   A print to
commemorate the feat hung in the dining-room,
and I had spent many an hour admiring the bulk
of the vessel, crowded with troops, and of the line-
of-battle ships blazing into each other from their wall-
like sides.   A man-of-war, to my mind, was a
floating castle, with banners and streamers, and
figure-heads and stern-galleries—like those in the
print, and in the pictures of "sea fights," by the
Dutch painters, in the gallery at the Castle—towering above the waters, with rows of ports and grinning cannon-mouths.   And now, as I looked in a
line with Window's forefinger, I doubted my
senses as I beheld a craft, the size of a fishing-
smack, as I thought, about a mile away from
us, with foresail aback, and mainsail loose, which
lay rising and falling on the swell, and showing
us at every rise the sheen of her burnished copper.
" Well, and what do you think her, my lad?"

"Isn't she very little, sir?" I faltered out.

"Little? Why she's the largest cutter in the service, my boy; one hundred and ninety tons, and as good as ever was built. Wait till you get on board. Feel at all queer, my boy?"

The expression of my face referred to my disappointment at the size of H.M.C. *Merlin*, rather than any other internal discomfort. When I stood on the broad, white deck, and looked at the huge mast, and the ponderous boom, I was somewhat comforted, and my peace was perfectly restored when, after an inspection of my cabin, which was a miracle of contrivances and neatness, I patted the long eighteen-pounder forward, and caressed the carronades which formed the broadside guns of the little craft. In a few moments more the uneasy sensation, and the motion which obliged me to catch hold of ropes, or gripe Window's brawny fist, was exchanged for a buoyant, gliding feeling, as the *Merlin*, clothed in her whole suit of snowy sails, careened over, and bowled past the Light-house with a fair breeze on the quarter. It was glorious! To watch the land recede, and the hills, in whose recesses glided my little trout stream, grow less—the Light-house and the long low wall extending into the sea, run by us, and the smoke over Dublin, become fainter—to skim past the laborious colliers and fishing-smacks—and then, as we slipped by the many-coloured Hill of Howth, and stood towards the south, to gaze on new scenes opening, and the expanse of sea growing wider still. Glorious, too, to see the green waves, with their creamy tops, coming on to meet us, like an army in battle array flouting its banners! glorious to drive them into confused flight of spray and water, and rush on to fresh encounters with the victorious cheering of the wind through our sails. Oh! terrible sea, you conquer in the end: beaten in the skirmish, you are dreadful and pitiless in the shock of battle.

"'Pon my word, Terry, you'll make as good a sailor as any of us. How do you like it now?"

"It's delightful, sir; I'm so thankful to you. Only for this, I would have hated the sea, and feared it too."

"Well, this is fine-weather sailing, my boy; and I hope we'll have no worse, for your sake. Come down to dinner—it's ready now, and you ought to be ready for it. Mind your head. Mr. Tiller, here's a young friend, Master Brady, who is going to take a cruise with us, and you must give him

fine weather, for we are going to have a great haul
of fishes."

Mr. Tiller, and his chief, and I, had a most delightful afternoon. There was beautiful soup—
quite different from Mother Murphy's preparations
at Dr. Ball's—but it was not so much the excel-
lence of the soup, as the difficulty of getting it to
the mouth, which commended itself to me. There
was a Dublin Bay haddock, boiled chicken and bacon,
salt beef, and a roly-poly pudding; and then there
were Tiller's anecdotes of artful smugglers, and more
artful revenue-men, in which there was very little
bloodshed and a great deal of glory, set off by
Tiller in language which was evidently deprived of
a natural garniture of an imprecatory nature by
the presence of " Captain Window." Up on deck,
afterwards, it was of never-ending interest to look
through the glass, as soon as I had learned to use
it, at the objects on shore, and to pry into the
crannies of the Wicklow mountains, to watch the
people on the beach, to study the towns and
villages, to observe the signals to the cutter from
the coastguard stations, and to see our mute
speech fluttering up and down as the old quartermaster spelt out the messages and prepared the
answers. I went to bed at night, swaying on my

knees by the side of my cot as I prayed for those
at home, and in the depths of my heart breathed
the supplication that Heaven would preserve me
till I could penetrate the mystery of my life, and
fill the aching void in my heart.

It was a strange troubled sleep into which I
fell. It seemed as though I were awake, and that
the vessel gradually grew in height and breadth as
she ploughed through the seas, which swelled
higher and higher, and rose over her deck, till at
last the beating waves rushed over us like mountains, but could not keep the *Merlin* in their power.
The sound of the sea as it swished by my pillow,
separated from the power of death by a few planks,
was filled, 1 thought, with voices of crying and
lamenting. Looking out into the green depth,
I saw there were myriads of people floating in the
sea, and holding up their hands in supplication.
The waves were crowded with infinite multitudes
in white, wafted to and fro in the currents,
amid which long seaweeds were waving, and
monsters of awful form passed on their way in
and out of profound caves in the earth. Many
of these ghastly creatures, clutching the ship
as she passed, clomb over her sides and got
upon the deck, where they sat huddled to-

gether. Some came down into the cabin and sat by our little fire. I could not make out their faces they were so white and expressionless, shifting in feature and in colour every moment. But at last Mohun came down, shivering and wet, and by his side was a tall form swathed in snowy drapery. He pointed to me. My heart gave one great throb, ceased to beat, then struck the sides of its prison with mighty blows. The veiled woman came towards me, and, as I struggled to rise, she lifted her veil, stretched out her arms—ah ! that lovely face !—" Mother ! mother darling !" I cried, and leaped from my cot to meet her; but at the instant the vessel shook as though she would split. I was thrown on my face, and a deluge of water flooded the little cabin.

" Make fast the deadlights," shouted Window from the top of the companion. As I got to my feet he came towards the door, with the rays of the lamp shining on his tarpaulin hat, in a thick pea-jacket, on which beads of spray sparkled like diamonds, his whiskers heavy with moisture.

" Don't be frightened, Terry, my boy," said he, seeing me in my shirt; " go to your blankets again, and to sleep, if you can. But hold on tight by your eyebrows. We are in for a blow;

the glass has gone down like a shot, and while we were shortening sail the cutter took in a little more water than we wanted. But she's all snug now, and if you like to see what a good sou'-wester can do in the Irish Channel on a short notice, I have no doubt we'll be able to oblige you. Good night, my lad. Stea-dy—ah! There now, in you go—good night."

Instead of taking easy and rather short dips into the water as she had done, the *Merlin* was now in for very long plunges and very high flights. I watched from my cot the pier-glass over the little fireplace in the cabin rising higher and higher, till it seemed to be trying to stand over me. Then the glass stood still for a part of a second, as if to make up its mind what to do, and abandoning the effort to mount higher, began to slide downwards, sinking faster and faster, till I could look upon it at my feet. Then a determination to try again, set the polished surface and the lamp which was reflected in the centre on the ascent once more.

I watched and listened to the dull roar of the waters, and the soughing of the wind mingled with the thud of feet, till I fell asleep, and slept on amid the storm. A hand on my shoulder woke me, and Jack Window's big bright eyes and ever-genial smile glanced in on me.   He was still shiny with wet oil-skins, and dripping beard and boots as before; and as he swayed to and fro, it was easy to see the *Merlin* was yet hawking up and down in the seaway after her unknown prey.

"By Jove, Terry, you're a trump," he exclaimed; "I'm so glad you've stood it all so well.   It has been a snorter, and it's not over yet; but the glass is rising a little, and it's shifting now to the west, so we'll have it off the land, and it can't do us any harm.   I needn't ask you how you've slept. I had a few peeps at you after the capsize you got, and you're a credit to Dr. Ball and the Seven Sleepers.   And now it's time to rouse out and get breakfast.   The steward has got out your oldest clothes, and I've got some tarpaulins for you in case you'd like to look at what's going on outside presently."

"And did you get up to look at me?   How very kind you are, Mr. Window.   I am quite ashamed to give you this trouble."

"Up! my boy.   Why, do you think I could turn in such a night?   No; that's the worst of it in a small craft like this.   No relief for me. The captain here is his own first luff, keeps his own watch and every one else's.   It's a bad place to

lie-to in.   No end of great hulking Yankee liners
and East and West Indians running up with
such a good wind for Liverpool, not caring a
dump what they run over.   Not to talk of Irish
pig-boats and rascally steamers from and to all
parts of the world.   I'll get a good snooze presently; and when you're all right we'll have our
breakfast."

When I put my head above the companion, my
first impulse was to rush back to the cabin instantly.
A vast pile of water coming towards the little vessel
shut out all the sea beside, and left only visible a
grey sky, against which its broken fringe, crowned
with seething foam, stood out sharp and distinct, as,
like some hill-side green and steep, it appeared to
roll down on the cutter.   But the good sea bird,
just dipping her beak into its base, fanning her tiny
wing of canvas, mounted the steep side—up, and up,
till she rode midst the hissing foam, and then
balancing herself with a slight shiver, and a heave
forward, as though she were about to leave the
sea, swooped down the other side of the billow,
eager to meet its fellow fast following in its course.
It was scarcely possible to believe I was on board
the same ship.   The *Merlin* had moulted her snowy
plumage—her topmast was struck, jib-boom run in,

and two tiny sails, wet and dark, represented the volumes of canvas in which she had been clad so gloriously. The smart man-of-war's men, whom I had seen yesterday in turn-down collars, flowing duck trousers, and dandy jackets, were now represented by a few uncouth-looking fellows in heavy jack-boots, with oilskin coats and sou'-westers, crouched down under the bulwarks, or anxiously watching the seas as the helmsman met the rise and fall. From the summit of each wave the scene was ever the same—a circle, with ragged margin, enclosing a raging, tumultuous mass of watery hillocks topped with white, all moving in order onwards, with valleys cleft deep between, the same cold grey sky as a background to fantastic cloud-shapes hurrying on ghost-like as if running races with the waves beneath.

"Is this a hurricane, Mr. Window?" I asked; "it is very awful."

"Lord bless you, this is nothing. It is a strong sou'-wester, that's all. It has come on very suddenly; but, as there was some sea before, there's a pretty run on. It's something more than a strong breeze, and perhaps it's a good half gale of wind. If we were in the old *Ramillies*, or even my old pet the *Phaeton*, we'd feel it more, I promise you. There's nothing like a roomy cutter for such weather; and the *Merlin* is as good a craft as ever Jack Window would like to be in— that is, for bad weather, my lad; for she's no good for pay, promotion, or what you call *kudos* in your school. Now, then, breakfast. We must do the best we can, as the cook can't work the galley very well."

And such a breakfast! How the little table was made to look like a window without glass, being covered with a framework, into which our crockery fitted! How my coffee, instead of going into my mouth, was shot down my neck! What desperate work it was to keep in one's seat, though it was bolted to the deck! What infinite delight I took in seeing the Lieutenant holding on to the table, at one time bobbing his head half across it, and the next nearly hitting it against the side! How very clever it was of the steward to take advantage of the pauses in the general unsteadiness, and to make a little run with *petit pas* steps, holding a dish in each hand, and to bring himself bolt up, and with an eye on each dish, and his feet apart, to sway gently over to counteract the roll of the ship; and then take a bend to the other side, till he could make good his landing in the cabin! All these things, and many others, made that marine breakfast most agreeable to me, not to speak of the unknown condiments and edibles fished out of tins, and canisters, and jars of many shapes and sizes.

Mr. Tiller looked in, very like a huge slug, so shiny and black was he.

"The glass is not what I'd like to see it yet, sir," he said. "I think we're in for a little more of it."

"Only for my friend here, whom I've taken out for a pleasure cruise, I don't suppose it makes so much difference to you or me, does it?"

"For pleasure, did he?" said Mr. Tiller, looking at me with evident pity. "He hadn't heard the proverb about those who go to sea for pleasure, I suppose, then? Pervided there was more sea-room, he'd not do badly, would he, sir, for a beginner? It's hard to tell where we are, and there wont be much chance of getting a look at the sun to-day."

"Perhaps we'll see the land," said I, innocently.

"God forbid!" exclaimed Mr. Tiller. "The worst thing could happen us, unless hitting on it without seeing it."

Mr. Tiller was right. The weather became

worse instead of better; and the wind, veering round towards evening, brought up a cross sea, in which the *Merlin* laboured frightfully. I could see by the face of the good Lieutenant that it was no laughing matter when a thump and a squashing sound announced the breaking of a wave, which rushed over the deck. The wings of the cutter had been pared and cut down to a mere feather, which, wet and strained to the utmost, seemed bent on flying away altogether, and pulled at the stays in desperation. Nothing so much astonished me as our solitude. I knew we could not be very far from land on one side or the other. Then we were in the highway of ships in the channel, and yet not a sign of one appeared on the surface of the storm-riven shield. When night set in, the tempest raged more furiously than ever. I began to understand how hard must be the life of men whose business is on the waters. In the darkness of my little manger-like cot I lay awake, watching the lamp in the saloon through the door-way swinging to and fro, and listening to the howl-ing of the wind and the never-ceasing rush of the sea—my thoughts for ever wandering to that Indian shore where all was hidden. The morning came; and, haggard and worn, with bloodshot eyes, my poor Lieutenant greeted me with his cheerful smile.

"It is well you slept so soundly, Terry. It blew great guns, I can tell you—nearly a gale, my lad. But the wind has suddenly fallen; the sea will soon follow it. You never stirred during the row on deck, when the big steamer came down on us; passed us two boats' lengths off in the middle of the hardest blow."

The sea was a long time going down, I thought, but towards evening we saw the land on our starboard bow. At nightfall we were running down towards a light, which began to show in the gloaming, flashing out and disappearing, and flashing out again; and as I turned in, the Lieutenant announced we would be in smooth water and lie snugly inside Carnsore in the morning.

"It is most provoking, Terry. I don't know what Doctor Ball will say to me," said Jack at breakfast, "but I have been signalled from the Coastguard Station to go round to Cove for orders. There must be something up, I expect, and I can't land and send you from this fag end of the world to Dublin by yourself. There is no mistake about it."

Mr. Tiller made his appearance at the cabin door.

" They're at it again, sir. They have just signalled for the cutter to stand in, as they want to communicate, and will send off a boat.

" In other words, Old Grubb wants a yarn, and anything else he can get on board. Run in as close as you can, and call me when he's within hail. Even half an hour or so will refresh a fellow who's been without sleep so long as I have, just enough to make him wish for the other seven hours."

We were closing in towards the land, which was marked by a belt of foam, and the surf pelting the base of rocky bluff. Above the line of black and white rose the green hillocks, which gradually faded into the purple haze of the mountainous background; and in a cleft in the strong battlements behind which the land resisted the encroaching sea, the bright whitewashed Coast-guard Station, with many little flags flying from the signal-staff, was visible. A speck on the waters, rising now on the top of a billow, and now lost for an anxious interval, could be made out with the glass; and as the cutter, fast running up sail after sail to make way against the ebb in the faint wind, rolled and lurched, yawed in the trough of the sea, and wabbled about on the top of the waves, there was a thumping of blocks and a flapping of canvas, a creaking of bulkheads, and general un-steadiness about us, which made the calm seem more dangerous than the storm, and gave me the idea that the *Merlin*, having become hopelessly upset in her behaviour during the last four-and-twenty hours, was determined never to become a sensible, well-regulated cutter again.

"Did you catch him that time, Grummett?" asked Mr. Tiller of the old Quartermaster, who, with one arm round a rattlin and the other propping the telescope against a shroud, was watching the progress of the boat.

"No, Mr. Tiller.   I saw Mr. Grubb plain enough in the starn-sheet, but I couldn't make out the other."

"Steady!   Here she comes again.   Ah! it's my opinion as it's the commodore himself is coming aboard."

In a short time all doubt on the subject of the illustrious visitor's identity was dissipated, and the Lieutenant roused up and went on deck to receive Captain Dumbleton, C.B., chief of all revenue cutters and coast-guards, and their belongings.   It was no easy matter to do so, for the cutter rolled savagely in the swell, and Captain Dumbleton was not formed for feats of agility.   But after a good deal of approaching and sheering-off, fending off and laying hold and letting go, a line was made fast to the Coast-guard boat, and presently the good-natured potentate was on the deck of the *Merlin*, followed by the gentleman I had heard designated as " Old Grubb," who was another stout mariner, with a broad red face and rheumy eyes, and much difficulty of breathing.

" I never was so pleased in my life, Window, as when we made out your number this morning! The *Sarah Sykes* has made her appearance again! Before it came on to blow I ordered them at all the stations to send you down at once, but I never expected you so soon. The *Hawk* left last Thursday night for Cove; the *Barnwell* has orders to communicate with her, and as you are so handy we really ought to catch her now."

" The *Sarah Sykes!* Indeed, sir."

" Yes. Was seen on Wednesday off the Black Bank; we have heard she left Treport, on her return from America, with a full cargo. That scoundrel Driscoll is in command of her, and he swears he'll land it or fight it on shore; so I have brought you some extra hands, and we must see if we can't catch him this time."

And Captain Dumbleton, taking the Lieutenant

aside, talked to him in whispers, whilst Mr. Grubb and Mr. Tiller entered into a general conversation and gossip of a coast and coast-guard character, to which in my ignorance I paid no great attention.

"Brady, eh?" quoth old Grubb; "I wonder if he's son of Major Brady of Bradyville, the member for Sligo? I like being civil to Parliament people's sons. When my case comes before the House, it's as well to have them on my side, though I know if it's justice is to be done, I don't need help from anybody after that case is stated. And so, Master Brady, you've come to sea for a lark? Well, you can tell your father, Major Brady, when you see him, that you had a very nice excursion. Pray remember me to him. My name is Grubb—Grubb, of the Coast-guard. He'll know all about my salvage claim."

"My father," said I, "is not alive; and he was not Major, but Captain Brady."

"Captain Brady? I knew him too. He was member for Cashel, wasn't he? As good a fellow as ever stepped."

"No, sir; my father was a member for no place. He was in the King's Own, and died out in India."

"The very man, I'm sure! Wasn't his father

member for Leitrim ?   I knew both him and his son, and I must have known your mamma very well.   If I am not mistaken, she was sister to Sir Thaddeus Standish, the member for Clare, and——"

"Mr. Grubb," interrupted Captain Dumbleton, who had overheard the last part of the speech, "I'm sure we are about to get on that Parliamentary question ; and as I have never been able to tell my county member the full particulars, perhaps you would wait till we get on shore."

"My mother's name was not Standish, at all events.   It was Billing," rejoined I ; "she was drowned when the *Ross-shire* East Indiaman went ashore on the coast of Ceylon."

"To be sure ! to be sure !" continued Captain Dumbleton.   "You and I remember it well.   You were in Galle, Window, in the *Calypso*, and I was at Penang, in the *Siren*, at the time ; and I recollect people saying how odd it was that those poor people were lost, and that it was said your mamma was seen alive afterwards."

Stretching out my hands I cried—

"Oh, for pity's sake ! tell me, sir——" when a roll of the cutter caused me to lose my balance. Ere I could catch at anything to save myself, I was thrown against the railing of the low bulwark.

There was a sound as of voices infinite in my ears, and a rushing, as if of life with a thousand feet, towards the portals of its prison. I was a good swimmer; and as soon as the shock was over, I turned and struck up for the green light above me. But what is this which settles on me like a wall, bars out the light, and presses me down and down beneath the cruel waters?

* * * * *

"You had indeed a narrow squeak of it! I could not see you when I dived, and I don't think I ever was so happy in my life as when I rose, and heard them sing out from the cutter that they had you. My poor boy!—what would I have done? But what signifies that? What would your grandfather and all your friends have done, if you had been drowned under my very eyes? Thank God, my boy, thank God! I never will, I swear, take man, woman, or child on a cruise again!"

The voice was dear old Jack's, as he sat beside me in my cot.

I had come up under the counter at the opposite side of the cutter, and as the *Merlin* heeled over she pressed me down, and was drowning me, when the next roll liberated me, nearly lifeless as I was ; I was just seen in time by one of the men in the coast-guard boat, who, with a lucky thrust of the boat-hook with which he was fending off, grappled my clothes and hauled me to the surface, where I was secured and hoisted on board, rubbed, and dosed with brandy, and covered with blankets, till I began to undergo the horrors of "coming-to," from which I had emerged as Jack sat with my hand in his, and his arm under my head.

"And now we must do the best we can. The Commodore, as we call him, would not wait, as soon as he saw you were all right, or I would have sent you on shore and trusted him to restore you to the arms of Dr. Ball. We are running down the coast, keeping a sharp look-out for a rascally smuggler—the only real one of the sort we have had to deal with for many a year—a Baltimore clipper, sailed by one Mr. Driscoll, an Irish American—and if it falls to my lot to sight the gentleman he wont find it easy to escape. It's not glorious work, Terry, but it may do me good—and God knows I want something to do that."

In the evening, when I got upon deck, the sun was sinking over the hills of Waterford, and cast its last beams over the heaving sea, which still felt the passion of its conflict. The brown-faced sailors, once more in their blue jackets and easy dress, seemed half inclined to cheer me as my curly pate rose above the companion hatch; and Mr. Tiller, who had been assiduous in his attention, bobbing in and out of my berth all the day, gave me a squeeze of his paw which set my fingers tingling with pain. When night fell, the *Merlin,* in smoother water, kept close in shore with a fine favouring breeze. I was fast asleep—too tired for dreams.

Heavens! what is that? The cutter has gone on a rock and we are lost! I was out of my berth and on deck in an instant. The first glance told me that the *Merlin,* under a mighty spread of canvas, was tearing through the sea far from shore. Some unusual event was taking place which had summoned all the crew forward except Mr. Tiller and the man who was steering.

Jack, glass in hand, was looking out by the side of the old quartermaster, who had screwed his eye into the end of the large telescope, and was on one knee peering into darkness. The men of the watch were all looking in the same direction. There was a strange sulphurous smell hanging about the deck, and two of the sailors were training one of the guns on our broadside up to the port again.

Mr. Tiller was rubbing his hands in great delight. "There'll be luck, after all, if we lay hold of her full of brandy and baccy, and maybe silk. I do think you may have brought us in fortune's way after all. Steady, Perks, steady; I'd give her something solid this time, to make her see we'll stand no nonsense."

It was the report and concussion of the gun fired with a blank charge over my head, which had roused me from my slumbers.

As Mr. Tiller spoke, a blinding flash lighted up the deck for a moment, and the carronade hopped in its carriage as it delivered the second angry message of the *Merlin* into darkness.

"Carrying on still, sir," cried a voice from the crosstrees, where one of the men was stationed, "and running up her gaff-topsail."

"By Jove, then, we must talk to her in earnest. Grimston, clear away the bow-gun, and give her a shot pretty close to her bows."

By dint of hard looking and the guidance of many fingers I could make out a schooner, which seemed to me somewhat larger than the *Merlin*, running on the same course as ourselves, but well to windward.

"I can't see anyone on her decks," whispered

Window, " except that fellow beside the steers-man; but I dare say there's a pretty nest of vagabonds on board, for all that. She's drawing on us, by Jove; has her sails flat as boards. Now to stop her capers. Are you ready there, Grimston ?"

" Ay, ay, sir; all right here. We want to fall away a point, if you please, sir, to shave her nicely."

And as the *Merlin* fell off I saw old Grimston take another look along his sights. The lanyard was pulled. Again the flash lighted up the eager faces—the *Merlin* quivered from the shock, and ere the crashing roar of the eighteen-pounder had well smitten our ears, the rush of the shot through the air boomed in a long hollow sound, tapering as it wore away till it was lost.

" Well done, Grimston ! Well done indeed ! Not twenty yards in front of her cutwater, I should think, at the second ricochet," shouted Window. " Hang me if the fellow minds us a bit. Phew— this smoke ! Aloft there. What's the schooner at ?"

" Running up her fore and aft staysail, and keeping on the same course, sir."

" We've lost by this trifling. This time we'll

show you we're in earnest, my man. Let her have it right across the beam, and if a spar goes she's only herself to blame."

Again the long gun spoke out. In a few seconds a suppressed exclamation from the men told the ball had missed its mark. The schooner still held on, and under her additional canvas was flying fast ahead, whilst the *Merlin* had lost way in yawing to train her gun.

" I don't think she can stand a stitch more canvas, sir," said Mr. Tiller, " if we were to carry all away. The wind is rising again as it is."

" Try her again, Grimston. I'll lay the gun myself." Window, full of the excitement, proceeded to cover the imperturbable schooner, now pronounced without doubt to be the *Sarah Sykes*, of Baltimore, U.S. Just as the lanyard was pulled the cutter gave a quick lurch; the shot striking far short of the schooner, threw up a pillar of spray and was lost from sight.

" She's gaining on us fast. I would sink her if I could, for there's no chance of coming up with her ;" and Lieutenant Jack this time spoke with clenched teeth, and uttered something very like a strong objurgation. " Now then, Mr. Grimston, do your best this time. Plump it right into her."

Whether the distance deceived the old gunner or not, the shot again fell short. Window now directed the elevation of the gun and revised the aim. As the *Merlin* steadied herself for a moment, he gave the word " Fire." Once more the shot struck short between us and the schooner, and flew astern of her, as I could see through the telescope by the white splashes in the water.

The schooner careening over to the increasing breeze calmly took in her staysail, as if to mock our efforts. It was evident the *Merlin* was letting her slip out of her claws by firing at such long bowls. The chance of hitting her decreased—that of overtaking her would soon be gone altogether. Window determined to lay his course again, hoping that one of his colleagues might block the bold smuggler, and that the sound of the firing at sea would arouse the coastguard to signal to the stations to be on the alert.

" She's making for the French coast, I think," said Mr. Tiller, " though, then, as I say to myself, if that's her game, why does she keep so much to the west'ard ? Driscoll can't hope to run a cargo with us after him, and all the stations roused. Maybe it's her best point of sailing."

" Anyway, Tiller, it's too good for us," said Jack

Window. "How she is walking along, to be sure !"

And so with much reluctance he was obliged to give up his hope of crippling the "enemy," as old Tiller called her. With very small chance of overtaking her, he resolved to pursue and keep the schooner in sight at all events. To me the whole scene was "great fun." It was full of excitement. I thought little of the horror which would have been worked had one of the missiles crashed into that solitary craft, smashing up wood and iron and the miserable wretches who were cowering behind the bulwarks, and yet held on their course. I could not see the pale resolute man, with compressed lips and frowning brow, who, grasping the tiller, was looking now aloft to the draw of his sails, and now to the dark side of the angry cutter, from which, as the flash came, he might expect that he and his venture were about to meet their fate.

Morning was breaking when I went up to have another look at the *Sarah Sykes*.

"Where is she now, Mr. Window?"

There was a look of undisguised vexation on his face as he pointed out a snow-white speck far away on the horizon, which the morning light threw in relief on the clouds and sea surge.

"Running away from us hand over hand; and what's worse, my lad, she's making right down Channel as if going to run for Brest—maybe across the Bay of Biscay. She is keeping away now from the Irish coast, and will, if she lies on her course, run pretty close to the Land's End. I can't lose sight of her, for Mister Driscoll knows what he's about; if he could dodge us he would very likely 'bout ship and make another run to land his cargo, knowing well the cutters are nearly all down about here. Confound you," continued he, shaking his fist, "I'll follow you till you're inside your bounds as long as I'm afloat. Well, it's a longer holiday than we reckoned on. There is every sign of another breeze of wind springing up, and if it's a rattler we may run down on him after all."

All day at sea—the centre of the shield on the outer rim of which, glinting like the wing of the mew, danced in the growing roll of the waves the object of our pursuit! Ships came in sight and sank beneath the horizon here and there, but every eye was turned on that tiny speck. And as night set in, and the wind rose still higher, and the *Merlin* lay over under a press of canvas, which made every spar scream as if in suffering, whilst the foam bubbled along the top of her lee bulwarks, Jack

Window, very anxious, and rather more stern and curt than I had seen him, held a council with his trusty aide, the result of which was that they would hold on in their pursuit, and that, if the *Sarah Sykes* got away, it should be no fault of his.

"If she was to lie-to now, I don't see what harm we could do her, supposing Driscoll has any papers at all. He might say he was going from Baltimore to Brest, and that he took a fancy to come round by the North Passage. As he's up to every trick on the cards, I can only suppose he has no papers to clear himself. He was certainly inside the line when we sighted him, and he refused to lie-to when fired at. No, depend on it, he is playing some deep and desperate game—something more than a mere affair of tobacco and brandy."

And so Jack sat over his rum and water ruminating, and looking at the glass from time to time, and cheering up as he saw it falling—for after a temporary rise the mercury began to go down again. He rubbed his hands now and then, and with an inquiring glance at Mr. Tiller, murmured, with an air of satisfaction, "We may catch him yet—we may catch him yet. I'll carry on till the sticks are in danger, I can tell you, Tiller."

And so he did. That night was terrible. Before

it was over, the *Merlin* was plunging in a sea of which the roll was grander and deeper than that I had witnessed with so much awe. As the gale grew in strength the cutter proved the correctness of the Lieutenant's prophecy, or at least of his hopes, and the distance between her and the schooner was obviously diminishing; but the *Sarah Sykes* altered her course towards evening.

"I'm darned if she's not going back to Amerikey, as certain as I live," grunted the old sailor at the helm; "we're going to have a spree in the Atlantic, young gentleman."

The Lieutenant's lips closed tighter than ever, and his brow darkened, as the sky, descending on the sea, poured forth its deluges of rain, and the wind tearing off the foaming summit of the billows blew them in flying scud over the boiling waters. Still, when the day was over, and the night came, the schooner was there. When the morning dawned she was still in her place. Men shook their heads. Mr. Tiller confessed to me, as we sat below, he would have been glad if she disappeared. "As long as she kept on her present course, the *Merlin*," he said, "had no chance; and if the wind went down again the schooner would just slip away again like a greyhound. Supposing the *Merlin* should come up with her in such a seaway, no boat could board her; and I don't suppose Mr. Window would venture to sink her."

He was interrupted in his confidences by the appearance of Window's head in the cabin. "I say, Tiller," he exclaimed, "the fellow has, just out of sheer bravado, run up the Yankee flag in blue water. We can just make it out—stars and stripes, sure enough, as big as a mainsail! But I'll make him show his papers, as I live."

"Yes, that's all very well, sir; but have we the right? We can't board him at sea, as we're only revenue, you know."

"There's the pendant flying," exclaimed Window, "and right or wrong I'll call Mr. Driscoll to account."

But the passion and determination of man were rebuked by the voice of the storm. The gale increased to a hurricane. The sea, almost beaten down by the force of the wind, had a fearful strength. Again and again ponderous sheets of water rushed over the staggering vessel, and strove as though they would fain press her down for ever. With topmast struck, her trysail reefed to a shred, and a tiny staysail, she struggled on like some drowning bird. At last it became evident that it

was madness to continue the contest with the Atlantic, and Window gave orders to lie to.   For
three long days and nights the *Merlin* rode in the
midst of the tempest ; and there, some four or five
miles away, rising and falling at long intervals in
the tremendous seas, lay the schooner, oftentimes
hidden from us by the scud and by the drift of the
tortured waters. All the time I, perforce, remained
in my cabin and in the little saloon, which had
become all my world, lighted only by the lamp
which burned night and day, with the hatches
battened and the dead-lights down. I could hear
the seas sweeping over the deck, and the tread
of the heavy boots above, and the thumping of coils
of rope ; the lamp swung backwards and forwards,
clicking like the pendulum of a clock, for ever
gathering a dank coat of salt dew, which crept
down below and pervaded all things ; the timbers
creaked and cried aloud, and little streams of
water trickling in and down over the paint, showed
how the *Merlin* was tried in the fight with her
enemy.   I was beginning to consider an angle of
forty-five up and down the normal condition of
marine life ; and our meals, such as they were, becoming worse every day, were eaten under circumstances of contrivance and dexterity almost incredi-

ble to the uninitiated. I knew we were in danger, though I could not tell what it was, for I saw Merry, our steward, crying and praying, and drinking a great deal of rum and water; and although the latter was natural enough, the former practices were not at all usual with him, as I had heard him more than once larding his speeches to little Dan, the captain's boy, with words which made my hair stand up. Window confessed it was the worst weather he had ever met in these parts—it was as bad as a hard cyclone, and nothing could stand it except such a boat as we were in, and "that confounded Yankee."

"And where is she now, sir?"

"She is—will you believe it, Terry?—she is actually quite close to us. We have never lost sight of her all this time, night or day. There's not a soul to be seen except one man on deck, and she is lying-to as comfortable as a duck. You don't know what absurd fellows sailors are. I declare there are some old salts on board who, I'm told, have quite a fear on them about her, and think she is not canny. I expect next they will swear she is the *Flying Dutchman.* No," he continued, "you must not go up yet: all hands are below whom we don't want. Stay here, my dear boy, and put your trust in Him who watches over the sea and land.   You are a brave, stout heart, and, with God's blessing, we will live yet to talk over the time that Jack Window nearly went down with you in the mid-Atlantic in a mad chase after that craft of the evil one———"

"That the craft and subtlety of the devil be brought to nought, good Lord deliver us," ejaculated a voice, with a hiccup, from the pantry.   Window, who knew the source of the sound, clenched his fist and his teeth.

"You'll catch it for this, Mr. Merry, I can promise you."

"Catch it !—and don't you call this catching it ? Oh ! Mr. Window, hear me entreat you to give up drink and bad company !   Give peace in our time, O Lord."—The prayer was interrupted by a cut over the shoulders with a strap, delivered by the Lieutenant with all his might, and Mr. Merry, who sat on the floor of his pantry, with a glass of grog in one hand, and with the leg of the table clutched in the other, then relapsed into a crying fit, and then prayed at intervals in a voice which became more inarticulate, till it graduated into snoring.

The gale moderated at the end of the third day.

The schooner shook out her feathers. Once more the chase was resumed, but with no better fortune. Day after day passed, one like another : the thumping of the waters against the much-vexed sides of the cutter—the words of command—the rattling of halyards and sheets on the deck, mingling for ever with the moaning and whistling of the wind— all around us a tumultuous sea, above a leaden sky flecked with cloud-shapes, hurrying in a chase as futile as our own. There came into my head a hope that somehow or other we might get to India at last—for my geography was rather vague, and was perverted by sentiment. But all such happy delusions were knocked on the head by old Jack, whom I began to tell all my thoughts to without reserve. The *Merlin* was fast approaching the shores of the New World.

"We are on the Banks and rather astonishing the cod-fishers, I can tell you, Terry. I fear I shall be beaten after all, be laughed at, and, what is worse, be reprimanded for leaving my station."

There, far as the eye could reach, were ships of all sizes and rigs lying at anchor in deep water, tossing and pitching in the roll of the sea; and as we passed close by a brig which was tumbling about in an agonizing manner, I could see the fishing-lines over her sides, and the men pulling up the cod-fish hand over hand from the depths below. Ahead of us ever was the schooner, flying through the maze of ships. The lights on board the fleet at night looked like lurid stars through the sea-haze.

"It is all over," said Jack to me, as I put my head out of my crib to inquire after the morning's news. "She is beating us fast, and land is in sight."

"Land!—what land?"

"Why the land of the New World, somewhere about Cape Cod, I guess, as the natives would say. There was just a chance that some of our cruisers from Halifax might be knocking about to look at the fishermen, or buzznacking for something or other, which might have helped me to lay hold of that slippery fellow. But no such luck. It's merely that I like to stick to my word I am carrying on still; and soon we'll have to 'bout ship and make straight back across the Atlantic for Dr. Ball, T.C.D., and his young friends. You'll be able to spin many a tremendous yarn, wont you, Terry, about our cruise? I only hope the Doctor and your grandfather wont prosecute me for running away with you."

It was as Lieutenant Window said: the cloud

I could just discern resting on the sea in the early morning, became more distinct and rose higher every hour, and spread away right and left; and fishermen, and coasting vessels with snowy sails, and all the signs of prosperous, busy maritime life, grew upon us; and at last we could see the villages, the white houses, and the churches on the land.

"The schooner is lying-to, sir," cried the look-out man; and there, sure enough, was the *Sarah Sykes* slowly coming round with her broadside to us. In another moment a puff of smoke rose from her side, and as it cleared away, we could see an enormous ensign at her peak—the stars and stripes, flying over a green flag. She was making signals to a sloop-of-war which lay in shore, and presently the latter filled her topsails and came down towards the smuggler.

Jack and Mr. Tiller were watching these proceedings through their glasses with an air of intense dissatisfaction. " I only want to give him a bit of my mind, but he will have the best of me; and he's signalling to that swaggering Yankee to come and help him to bully us. I swear I shouldn't be at all surprised if the fellow pretends to have grounds of complaint against us. It is enough to make a man mad, to be led such a wild-goose chase —to be laughed at on this side of the Atlantic— to be near foundering with all on board in the middle of it, and to be certain of coming to grief when I get to the Old World.   However, there's no help for it.   Mr. Tiller, I shall put about now, for I am not in a humour to stand any of their chaff, and perhaps something worse.   No! no!— haul down!" he exclaimed angrily, as the Union Jack was running up; "haul down at once."

By this time the sloop-of-war and the schooner had come within a mile of each other, and as the *Merlin* put her bow eastward, we could see a boat push off from the latter and make the best of her way towards the man-of-war.   The wind had fallen light in shore, while there was still a fair leading breeze outside, and the cutter, on her best point of sailing, went buzzing through the water at the rate of twelve knots an hour.

"It's no use, my friend!   It is our turn now!" quoth Jack Window, with a little touch of his old smile on his face, as he stood looking over the taffrail, with his glass to his eye. "If you want to catch us you must send the schooner after us, and I only wish you would dare, that's all; I'd give a year's pay to see it."   And in effect the sloop, with all sail set, and a number of signals to which she called attention by gun after gun, seemed to be anxious to overtake the *Merlin*. But she did not; and as the moon rose in the first cloudless sky we had seen for many a night, the man-of-war was hull down, and in the morning was gone altogether.

Sixteen long days and nights at sea! How I began to hate the biscuit and the salt pork, and beef and beans, and brown-black coffee, although whales, and porpoises, and albecores, and gannets—nay, a devil-fish and a veritable shark—came to diversify the voyage. The strain and the excitement were all gone. Jack Window was busy with logs, and journals, and writing reports—the latter were never-ending, still beginning, and mostly went fluttering away in fragments over the side.

" I would sooner write a despatch about a general action," he groaned. " Oh! how they will pitch into me !" And I sat and looked at him and sighed to think that I could not help him. There was but a limited library on board—the " Nautical Almanac," " Navy Lists," " Coast-guard Regulations," " Orders in Council," " Nories' Navigation," a collection of Board of Trade and Custom-House circulars and memoranda, " The Life of Nelson,"

" The British Worthies " — an odd volume of " Hakluyt," which was my mainstay. But before the voyage was half done I had finished " Hakluyt," and the " Worthies," and " Nelson," and had ventured on " Norie" and Navy Lists. Sometimes it occurred to me that Dr. Ball would be rather angry, and that my grandfather would be fretting for my absence, and perhaps uneasy ; but I never supposed that there were any downright fears for our safety. It was nearly a month since I set out on my eventful voyage. I could not then—for I had never felt it—imagine how watching and waiting fill the soul with gloom and bury hope at last.

CHAPTER VIII.

" WE are all so glad to welcome you, old fellow —not a soul ever expected to see one of you alive again. Why, it's famous!" And Captain Buddicombe, who stood on our deck as the *Merlin* brought-to under the guard-ship, off Spike Island, in Cove Harbour, shook his old shipmate by the hand again and again.

" Lost! why, what else could we think, my dear Window? It is now the 4th of May. You were last seen off Ballycotton on the evening of the 5th of April. There was one of the worst gales we have had on the coast for years. The Cove, and Youghal, and Kinsale men tell us they never knew a heavier sea on. A vessel dismasted, which looked like the cutter, was seen to go down in the height of it off the Seven Heads. Next day, a larger craft, which had been seen in her company, came ashore at

12

Horse Island, and was of course broken up into firewood; but it was evident she was American-built.   She was laden with rum, brandy, tobacco, and French silk; a piece of her stern-board, with the letters ' *a,h, S,y,k,*' in gold, was washed ashore, and a part of a boat, with the letters and words ' altimore, U.S.,' on it.   The bodies that were found could not be identified, but Rattray says, from their clothing and marks, they were mostly Frenchmen and foreigners.   It was known you were chasing the *Sarah Sykes,* and putting one thing and the other together—although there was great faith in the sea-going qualities of the cutter — when days lengthened into weeks, and still there was no sign of you, the most hopeful agreed there could be only one conclusion.   All the papers have been full of the 'Loss of her Majesty's cutter *Merlin,* J. Window, Lieutenant R.N., commanding, and all hands.'   We welcome you as one who has come back from the grave."

Jack Window, with his eyes wide open, listened to the captain, and when he had done, putting the paper on his knees, he gave a very gentle and very long whistle.

" ' *A, h,*' that's the end of ' *Sarah,*' " quoth he ; " and ' *S, y, k,*' that's the beginning of ' *Sykes,*' on her stern ! ' a, l, t, i, m, o, r, e, U.S.,' which only wants a ' B' to be ' Baltimore,' on her boat ! Then, in the name of all that's wonderful, what have I been running after ?" He continued as if reading from a list :

" A schooner about two hundred and eighty tons, long and low in the water, with tall, raking masts, gilt figure-head a woman's face, fine bow and run, square stern, overhanging counter, coppered to the bends." " If ever a craft answered in all particulars to description, that Yankee I've been making a fool of myself after, is the *Sarah Sykes*, of Baltimore !" " Michael Driscoll, a deserter from the Royal Navy, native of Kinsale, and now citizen of the United States, master, sailing generally with clearances from Boston for Havre." Well, I know nothing about the last part, for they would not let me near enough to see them. Hum ! and so you all thought we were lost. Here we have it," and Jack Window began to read a newspaper where Captain Buddicombe's finger was resting. " ' Loss of his Majesty's cutter *Merlin*, and all souls;' that's good, to begin with. ' Regret to say—hum !—further accounts— hum !—confirm painful—hum !—total loss. Fine vessel—hum !—deserving, but over-zealous officer.' *Over*-zealous !—what's that ? ' Crew, forty-five souls ; widows, children—lament—hum——' " his face assumed an expression of pain; he read on silently—clasped his hands—let the paper fall at his feet—and looking at me with eyes slowly filling with tears, took me by the hand, and said—" Terry, my dear fellow, I have news for you. Come down with me to the cabin. Buddicombe, I'm sure you will excuse me for a few minutes; this is the boy who is mentioned—from Dr. Ball's—in the paper, whose grandfather you know—Dr. Brady. All right, God bless you. Come, Terry—come along. We have all our trials, and mine and yours began early."

There was something in his words and manner which made me anxious. I asked, " Is there anything about grandpapa in the papers? Is he quite well ?"

" Quite well, Terry—quite well ; better than he has been for many a day." Jack Window was a bad dissembler ; I heard him cough in an odd kind of way ; the tears were stealing down his checks. " Don't ask me yet. We must see if it's true, my lad. Why here have they been quite sure that we have been all at the bottom of the sea for the last four weeks, and not a hair hurt in the whole crew ! Come what will, I must get leave, and we will go up to-night together by the Cork mail."

"But what is it that is not true? If grandfather is well, that is all right; what does the paper say, Captain Jack?"

"I will tell you by and by, Terry. You must not believe a word of their confounded story." I felt more uneasy than before. He continued—"You see the papers gave out that we were lost. Dr. Ball wrote to your grandfather to say you had been allowed to go with me on this unlucky cruise; and your grandfather, they go on to say, began to get frightened like the rest at the ridiculous story in the papers. Well, he comes to Dublin to see Dr. Ball, and then he goes to the coastguard stations, and worries himself. What is the use of all this talk, my dear boy? Here we are, within a few hours of Dublin. The boy is packing up your clothes. I have sent to engage places, and to-morrow I will restore you to the Doctor, and bear my punishment meekly."

"But what does the paper say about grandpapa? Why should anything be said of him? It makes me so miserable. Do tell me, because I must know."

Jack Window looked at me straight from his great eyes, and there was a tenderness in his tone as he spoke which sunk into my heart. "What is said is that your grandfather, Terry, has been very ill.   With us it would matter little whether an old country doctor was ill or well; but it's something to belong to what they call the 'old stock' here; and there are notices of your family as long as my arm, my dear boy, all turning on the supposed fact that you have gone down, in the thirteenth year of your age, in the ill-fated *Merlin*. They rake up all the old bones they can find of Generals, Barons, and Counts Brady and O'Brady. And, finally, they give the old gentleman a stroke of apoplexy in order to finish off their article. You may be sure it's not true.   But remember, Terry, that come what may, you must look on me as your friend.   I have little kith and less kin, and no friends but myself, and you are a mere boy, on the very outside of the race of life in which you see me winded and beaten; but it is something, nay, a great thing, to have a friend; and when you are a lion, if ever you get into a net, call on Jack Window, and you may reckon on teeth, and perseverance in the use of them."

It is one of the many happinesses of youth that its sorrow is not deep or lasting.   It is passionate—fervent, whilst it endures; but the sun soon breaks through the clouds.   It must be of youth that it is said " Sorrow endureth for a night, but joy cometh in the morning." So of the anticipations of grief, which make the bulk of the wisdom of old age; there is in youth but a slight leaven—too little, thank heaven, to leaven the lump. As I rattled away in the inside of the mail with Jack Window, who was full of documents and troubles, I had almost forgotten all my fears and grief, and had brought myself to believe with him that all these rumours of evil were as baseless as my night-dreams.

It was near nine o'clock next day before Jack and I, on an outside car, were on our way to the suburb of Dublin in which Dr. Ball's establishment was situated. Jack Window was very grave then. I had seen him speaking to a man in the Post-office yard, and noted that his face fell as he spoke; but as he got up beside me he took my hand, and said, "We're in time, my boy. Please God, all will be right yet." When we arrived at the old house Doctor Ball was standing at the door to welcome me, and the windows were filled with faces, for the news of our safety and of our coming had gone through the school. There was less stateliness and more kindness in the Doctor's manner than usual. He held out both hands to welcome me.

"Ah, Mr. Window, what a time we have had of

it !   We will hear the story of our young Ulysses presently, when he has seen his grandfather."

" My grandfather here !" I exclaimed.   " Oh, where is he ?   Let me go to him at once."

A quick glance passed between the Doctor and Window, and I heard the latter whisper, " I have not told him all about that."

" The fact is then, Brady," continued Dr. Ball, turning to me and dusting some snuff off his shirt-frill, " the fact is, your respected grandfather has been and is ill—so ill that the physicians order the greatest quiet and calm to be observed.   Nothing must be allowed to agitate him ; and we must break the news of your arrival here very gently, in the course of the day.   He has been in some degree prepared for good news—not without hesi-tation among the medical attendants—by being told some doubts are entertained if the vessel seen to go down was the *Merlin*.   Nothing can exceed the kindness of Sir Richard's household.   If she had been his daughter, Miss Butler could not be a better nurse—so tender, so thoughtful for her years. You must be patient, my young friend ; to-day is almost the crisis of his illness."

By degrees I heard the whole story.

Dr. Ball wrote to Lough-na-Carra to say he had

given me leave to take a sail along the coast for a couple of days, with a naval officer who had known my father out in India, and that he greatly feared some accident had occurred, as more than a fortnight had elapsed and nothing had been heard of the cutter; that there had been dreadful storms at sea soon after she was seen off Wicklow Head, and that there were reports of a wreck on the south coast. My grandfather posted up to town immediately. Then he went along the coast, travelling from one station to another, making inquiries and sifting the stories of the men and of the country people, till he came to the scene of the wreck, and to the place from which the *Merlin* was seen to founder. He had overtaxed his powers, journeying without intermission, walking among the cliffs. As he gazed on the sullen ocean beneath which his loved boy was sleeping for ever, the spark of hope dwindled and expired—nature gave way. The sailors who accompanied him to the spot had gone a little way off, for they heard his smothered sobs. When they turned, after a time, he was not in sight. They were horrified to find he had fallen over the cliff and was lying on the beach below, insensible, his white hair soaked in blood. For days he lay between life and death; but he was strong of frame;

his natural vigour of constitution came to his aid, his broken arm knitted well, and he slowly recovered the power of utterance. His sole wish was to be brought back to Lough-na-Carra. They heard him in his sleep speaking of some wicked woman who should never touch a farthing of the money; and tossing in troubled dreams, he cried for mercy for his grandson. They carried him on a litter to the beach, and he bore the passage round to Dublin, buoyed up by the desire to return to his home. Sir Richard Desmond insisted on taking the old man to his house in Merrion-square till he could continue his journey to Lough-na-Carra; and although he in the utmost grief told all his friends he did not care to live, he vowed at the same time he must get to his house ere he died. Two days before the *Merlin* appeared in Cove, as he was seated in his easy chair, his eye rested on a paragraph in the paper. He uttered a feeble exclamation : " My God ! she comes again !" and tried to rise. His servant ran to his assistance, but the old man was speechless and powerless. What it was he had seen to affect him so powerfully no one could say ; but his hand clutched the newspaper firmly, and he resisted all attempts to remove it from his feeble grasp.

This was what I heard with grief—not " too deep for tears." In my inner heart I blamed myself for being the cause of all the suffering which he had undergone.

I went over to Merrion-square with Jack Window at once, for the honest fellow had come back to bid me good-bye ere he returned to his ship. There was, as he expected, what he called " no end of a row.   Most likely he would be keel-hauled by the bigwigs; but it would be just as well, for he had only taken coastguard-service for want of something better; and he didn't much care.

" I will fix myself somewhere near you, Terry, when the old man gets well, and you get your vacation-time—somewhere near a trout-stream, and within sight of the sea; and, meantime, let me hear from you regularly and I'll tell you how every- thing goes on.   We will remain friends, wont we, Terry, though I've caused so much trouble?"   A silent grasp of the hand was my answer.

We had just turned into the square, near the corner of which Sir Richard's house was, and Maurice Prendergast was coming down the steps.   He had sat with me, listening to my adventures, in my room, and had thrown his arms round my neck and embraced me the moment he saw me; but he had never said a word of visiting Sir Richard Desmond; and now his face reddened, and he stammered and looked down when I exclaimed, "And so you were calling to see how grandpapa was! It is very kind of you, Maurice; I hope you have a good report."

"I was at Sir Richard's on business," he replied; "that is, I had to try to see him or Miss Desmond about a little matter my sister asked me to get done—something for her school. I couldn't see them, for they both left town this morning; and Miss Butler's gone, too. Dr. Brady is better, but still very bad."

"Will you wait, and we'll walk back together?"

"No, thank you; I have somewhere else to go to, and the Doctor has only given me leave for two hours;" and he walked away, with his quick step, and his hands in his pockets—there was likely to be little else in them—and his head down, as was his wont. And Jack Window stood looking after him, and walked up and down, as I made my inquiries. Vincent, the old porter, though he rarely visited the castle, knew me well enough, and waddling back to the fire in the hall, which was lighted in spite of its being a fine day in May, patted the coals, wheezing out his news.

"And that's how it is, Master Brady—'per-carious state,' was Sir Philip's words, 'but on the whole a shade of improvement,' says he. Sir Henry was for it that he was a power better, and Graves was for that, too; and they'd a great deal of learned talk just at the foot of the stairs there. But I'd back Sir Philip agin all of them. Anyway, the house is just like Madame Stephens', or Mercer's, with the doctors coming and going in their shoots of black, and their big gold watch chains, and their shining boots that makes no noise. But who'd grudge it if they'd get the darlint ould man all right again?"

"And Sir Richard and the family are gone, Vincent?"

"Oh, aye; one of their sudden moves. Not a word of it did Mounseer Pitty know last night; and Sir Richard had him up at cockcrow, and orders him to pack and be off—and little pity I have for the same conceited Frinchman. Mamselle, I hear, is goin' to give notice—her health can't stand these tremenjous stravagins. Poor Miss Desmond and the young missus had to be nimble, I can tell you. They've left Mrs. Whipple, the housekeeper, in charge, and she's in the ould gentleman's room this minit."

"Well, say I'll be back again this evening before dusk, and Dr. Ball will let me come whenever I like."

"I heard them saying you was to stop here as soon as your grand-dadda was better. It was Miss Mary put that in their heads, I know; but Sir Richard went off so smart he'd no time to think of it."

As I was walking back towards the house with Jack Window, who seemed as anxious as I was about a man he had never seen, I gave him all the particulars.

"Who was the lad you met just now, Terry," he continued, "as we were outside the steps?"

"A schoolfellow, Maurice Prendergast, son of a country gentleman near Lough-na-Carra."

"I don't know why, Terry, exactly, but somehow I doubt if he's a good fellow. I don't like to see a young chap like that so thoughtful and cautious-like. He's a handsome lad; but there's mischief in those deep-seated black eyes and those thin lips. I'm not more of a judge of men's phizzes than other people who go about the world on their own hook early in life, but I think his figure-head means danger. I must bid you good-bye. Our little excursion, which began so quietly, has grown into a great event; I hope it will have no results which will ever cause you to regret our fishing acquaintance. As a last word, I can only say I shall always look out for your future with interest, and hope to see you making a name for yourself. Don't," he said, after a moment's pause, "mind what I said about your schoolfellow, Prendergast. It's just as likely I'm wrong as right. Suspicion and distrust will come soon enough." Another shake of the hand and he was off; but it was only to turn round and impress on me to write, and not mind postage, and let him know how Dr. Brady got on. "I'll send you my address as soon as I know what they are going to do with me. Good-bye, Terence— God bless you; and remember you will ever have a sure, if feeble, friend in Jack Window."

The turn of the street hid his figure, as, with a light jerky step, he walked briskly away.

A few days had made a great change in my reflections. Care had come indeed. There was now a real potent cause of solicitude, which I felt was little akin to that fantastic uneasiness which had so long possessed my spirit. The good old man who loved me so, and who had watched over me with such tenderness! I might never see him more. I did not ask what would become of me; but

I was full of remorse at the idea that I had been, however innocently, the cause of his illness. My life was about to bear the mark which even youth must feel. Morning and evening I went over regularly for more days than I can remember. I heard the report of the doctors from Vincent or the servant, and sometimes from Mrs. Whipple herself, whose silk dress and white cap and collar were as angular and hard as the good creature herself was round and soft.   He was slowly—very slowly—recovering from the sleep so little separated from death — his consciousness returning, too — Mrs. Whipple thought if his mind could only be kept quiet he would soon get right.   But he was for ever distracting himself about all sorts of people. Mrs. Whipple opined they were creations of his brain : some woman, he thought, was coming to disturb him—to take his son from him, or his grandson—to come to Lough-na-Carra and destroy every one—a sort of witch she must be ; and then he raved so, poor gentleman, it quite put him back again.

One day Vincent, as he opened the door, had a pleasant look, which almost prepared me for good news.   " Sir Philip and all of them is agreed the squire, your granddadda, is a deal better this morning. Faith, it was wantin' to get up and go down to the country he was, poor gentleman, by the night mail. And Sir Philip says he'll be able to judge this evening if it's right to give him another dose of the same medicine. They're jist giving it to him by dhrops—in hints and scraps —at a time, and it's all about yourself, and that there are chances of your not being lost after all; they're coming on to the news by degrees, that you're alive and well—and faith, if he could see you this minute, Master Terence, I think it would do him all the good in the world, for it's well you look, and alive you are, and no mistake about it."

The first sick room makes a deep dent in the memory: the phials on the mantelpiece, the glasses and bottles on the table, the imperfect light, the constrained movements, the quiet noises which dominate the silence. I can see my grandfather now as when my eyes rested on him through the opening door—seated in an easy chair in his well-known old dressing-gown of faded blue velvet, with its tarnished silver cord; his white hair escaping from beneath a skull-cap, and one foot resting on a cushion; his cheek flushed and thin, his look excited and eager.

" And they actually said he would be here to-

night, Whipple?—the darling boy.   Thank God—
thank Him for that great mercy."   He was silent,
and one hand sought its fellow and pressed the
fingers as his face was turned towards heaven.

"Yes, indeed they did, Doctor.   And Sir Philip
said to me—'If he arrives to-night, and the squire
is not asleep, you may let the young gentleman
just come in to say good night, and go away again.
But tell my old friend,' said Sir Philip, 'I'll be
very angry if he keeps him longer than that.   It
will do neither of them any good.'"

"What time did they say he would be here?   If
he comes by the day coach he is very nearly here
now"—he examined an old gold watch on the table
by his side.   "Ah! it will make me quite myself
the moment he comes."   I heard his anxious inquiries—I could see his face—whilst Mrs. Whipple,
half turning to the door as if listening, with her
finger raised to impress on me the necessity of cau-
tion, controlled the situation.

Not long after that I was seated at his feet, with
my head on his knee, and his arms round my neck.
Alas! one poor hand was gathered up and cold, the
fingers bent and stiff, the arm numbed and scarce
capable of motion; his figure was inclined and
contracted at one side, his face rigid, and the

mouth curved downwards — he spoke with difficulty; but for me it was enough to be there—
to see him—to return the pressure of his hand, to
listen to the broken accents in which he spoke so
fondly.

The summer holidays were so near at hand by the
time the doctors considered my grandfather was
sufficiently recovered for the journey to Lough-na-
Carra, it was proposed to let me go back with him.
Was there ever a schoolboy who objected to a longer
holiday than he expected?

" Dr. Ball sees not the least reason why he should
not go; and," added Sir Philip, " he seems to be of
more service to you than any of us."

Every day, indeed, I had my visit to the familiar
room, and at last the old man was well enough to
get downstairs with a little help, and then, by degrees, he ventured on walking in the Square, leaning
on my arm—walking feebly with a painful effort.
A great change had taken place in him. We had
become more than friends. Ever since the eventful
cruise he seemed uneasy if I were away from his
side; and a few minutes' delay in my arrival put him,
as Mrs. Whipple said, " quite in a fluster." We
were never so happy as when he was sitting in his
easy chair, whilst I was crouched on a stool at his

fect reading some of my books, conscious that his eyes were resting on me, and feeling his hand on my shoulder.

The day of our return to Lough-na-Carra is another of my memories. We posted down from Dublin; and as the postboy led out the horses for the last stage, taking off his cawbeen to my grandfather, he exclaimed, " Long life to yer honour and to the young masther! They're all expectin' you in the town, so they are. God knows the poor has missed yer honour badly !"

And as we drew up to the " Desmond Arms," there, sure enough, were all the old people and the young assembled in the street, and the bells of the church were ringing, and the rector, and the priest, and the curates were ready to welcome the Doctor, and burst into a cheer as they saw his face in the carriage! But when he got down and limped towards the Lough-na-Carra carriage through the little crowd, silence came upon them, mingled with that smart clack of the tongue and short sucking of the breath which the Irish use to express pity and surprise. He was altered indeed! These little marks of sympathy and regard were too much for his enfeebled nerves; and as his hand was shaken by his neighbours and dependents, I felt his useless arm quiver on mine, and saw the tears stealing down his face.

" I thank you all, boys and girls, and you, my kind, good friends. You see I have brought him home with me; and there will be some fun in Lough-na-Carra perhaps again when I'm a little stronger."

Amid the " Amens" of the people the old mare, roused to unusual vivacity even for her by the cuts of the whip which old Dan gave unconsciously in his excitement, started off down the main street, and we sat together on one side whilst Dan directed his course amid pigs and children to the old lodge, and whirled up to the hall door, where all the servants were gathered on the steps to greet their master.

I could not help feeling as if I were to blame, and the secret compunction I experienced was sharpened by the reproachful expression which I fancied I could detect in the looks of the neighbours.

CHAPTER IX.

For a time it seemed as if the Doctor would recover his health, but the tokens of returning strength passed away, leaving him but a weak, uncomplaining invalid.   His face was restored to its usual outline; he could walk, and use his arm, but his gait was feeble and uncertain, and there was a vacant, dreamy sadness in his look and expression.   I observed the servants were infected by this melancholy.   Sometimes after the post came in my grandfather would appear more depressed than ever, and would stay in his room rummaging papers and writing.   Strange visitors came to the house, and saw him privately and went away.   The family lawyer, Mr. Bates, stopped with us for several days, and had long interviews with the attorney of Kilmoyle and the land agent.   The air was full of mystery and some gloomy influence which settled on us all; and oftentimes I could catch my grandfather's eye resting on me with such solicitude and compassion, that I was alarmed by the fears of an indefinite calamity impending over me, which were all the greater because of their vagueness. I used to steal away to my little room and wonder what it all meant, and look at the copy of my mother's picture over my bed, and then, under the ever-present sentiment which governed so much of my life, creep gently down to the great gaunt room, and gaze on the original of the portrait of her whom, without seeing or knowing, I so dearly loved.

It was one summer's afternoon, and my grandfather sat after dinner with Mr. Bates—I had come in from a ramble along the banks of the river, and was passing through the hall—when I heard Mr. Bates say, " I would tell him all about it at once. He is old enough to know the truth. Call him in, sir, and tell him. If you like, I will go out and leave you." I stood at the door, my heart beating violently, my lips open, my breast heaving.

My grandfather's voice was agitated and low.

" Yes, Bates; he should know all before I go. But why so soon? Why cloud his years so early? Poor boy, he has trouble enough before him."

I entered the room and said, with as much calmness as I could command, " Indeed, grandfather, I could better bear anything than to see you ill, and to suffer as I do from all kinds of fears. Try me, and you will see how I will bear it. I am strong and well; and if there is anything to tell, I feel it would do me good to know it now."

My grandfather's face had a puzzled, undecided expression. Mr. Bates sat, with his wine-glass to his eye, looking at the sunset through the mellow purple of the claret which half filled it.

" No doubt about it, my old friend; Terence is now going on for fourteen years of age—strong, and tall of his years too. It will all come out sooner or later; and the boy has his own suspicions all is not right as it is."

" Well! well!" sighed the old man; " Terry, go into my study and bring out my desk."

The old brass-bound rosewood desk, over which he sat so often, was before him in a moment. My grandfather selected the key from the bunch that hung from a black silk riband in his fob, opened the desk, raised the lid, and then, touching a spring which revealed a secret compartment, took out a bundle of letters. His hand shook, and a strange frown came to his brow, as he picked from the middle of the bundle a packet wrapped in oil-skin, which he slowly uncovered and examined, as though to make sure he was right. The contents were two letters, discoloured and yellow, on which the black wax of the broken seals was yet visible in patches; and I felt at once these letters were to me the solution of the mystery which had troubled me so long. He held out one of the two.

"Before I give you this letter to read, I have a few words to say. No, Bates—stay, if you please; you know all, and the poor boy will want your advice when I am no more. I would rather you stayed, indeed. Take this letter, Terry, and see if you can read the writing on the outside."

I took the letter in my hand, and saw, in a small clear angular hand—"Dr. Brady, Bradystown House, Lough-na-Carra, Kilmoyle, Ireland." In the corner was written "M. B." On the top—"To be delivered, on arrival, by Mohun." I read the address, and the Doctor resumed—

"That letter is from your mother, my child, the widow of my son, your brave and unhappy father. You have heard how he died in India, when you were very young; and you have heard, too, that your mother was drowned on the coast of Ceylon, when the ship in which she was coming to Europe after her husband's death, struck on a reef of rocks. I must go back a little. Your father was my only son. I had looked forward to the day when he might take my place in this old house here, marry one of his own people, and pass away in the arms of his children, long after my bones had been laid with those of our luckless race. Now I sit here, a poor, broken, desolate old man, with only you to comfort me, and all the hopes of my life lying in his distant grave. He went to India with his regiment after the usual routine of home service, and in the war which we were carrying on there he distinguished himself, so that he got his captain's commission for service in the field; and everything went so well with him I began really to think—as you may remember, Bates—that there was some gleam of good fortune in store for us, and the thought set me working all the harder to clear Lough-na-Carra for him, and to get the property out of the difficulties which seem entailed on the land. I needn't trouble you with that yet, Terry. From all sides I heard good accounts of my poor boy—how gallant he was, how gentle and good, how simple and how noble. Every one spoke well of him, and my heart was filled with thankfulness to the Almighty who had so blessed me with a son.   Every letter that I got went to the Castle, where the eyes of Mary Desmond grew brighter as they rested on the lines—every paper in which his name appeared, and every account I heard of him, found its way to the Castle; for although the Desmonds are great people now compared to us, it was understood that there would be no objection to your father's marrying the lovely girl whom we all believed he loved with an affection equal to her own.   Her father would not hear of a regular engagement, nor would he let them correspond; but he always said he would make no objection to the match.   His son, the great Indian civilian, wrote home to say there was not a finer fellow in the service than Jack Brady, and that he heartily approved of the match of which he had heard.   All this time there was no promise on either side, but there was an understanding which we all looked on as certain.   Where could he meet a girl so good, so beautiful, so suited to him in every way as she who remained at her father's in this dull old place, instead of going to balls and parties and enjoying herself, and gracing the society of which she would have been the highest charm, all on account of him? I was quite happy then; and even Dick Butler's importunity, and his avowed determination to marry his cousin Mary, and his reckless bets and restless manœuvres did not cause me a moment's thought. Oh! how I counted the days for his return. His time for leave would soon be up. One day—one day—it was little more than two years before you were born, Terry—a letter came to me in that well-known hand. It contained news which pained and surprised me. Not a word had come to prepare us for the news that your father was going to be married, and here was a letter under his own hand to say that he had met a young lady at a ball at Cawnpore a short time previously, and that he was happy to say they were just going to start for the hills to spend the honeymoon—words could not do justice to her exquisite beauty—she was the loveliest being in India, and he was looked on as the luckiest fellow in the service; true she had no money, but her father was an old officer of long standing; and then he went on to describe his happiness, and the charms of this child of sixteen, who was, he said, more like twenty years of age, as she had been born and educated in India. A paragraph in a newspaper confirmed this dreadful surprise. I could not go near the Castle—the thoughts of meeting Mary Desmond were too terrible. But the poor girl knew as well as I did when the Indian letters arrived at the village, and that evening, as I was thinking how I should break the news, the wheels of her little pony-carriage grated outside the hall door, and ere I could escape she was standing with a blush and a smile on that frank face, which reflected every feeling of a soul in which there was no guile or shadow of turning. Ah! Bates—the torture and shame of that moment. Her quick eye at once detected my agitation—one hand was pressed against her heart as she put her arm round my waist, and sinking her head on my shoulder, whispered—'Is he ill? Tell me, or I shall die.' Let me pass over that interview. She would not be refused. I was in such a state of uneasiness about her increasing agitation—unusual in one generally so calm and collected—that in very fear I broke the news to her by degrees, and she heard it all with her face buried on my breast, and her fair arms twined round me, with a sudden stillness which from the moment I commenced the story, was only broken by my voice and the labouring of her poor heart. When all was over, she asked me to let her see the letter. I handed it to her, and taking it from me she arose and walked with it to the window, as the light was failing. At the end my poor son had written—'Tell Miss Desmond of

my happiness, and assure her how glad I shall be
to hear that some fortunate fellow has secured her
fair hand, though I do not think any man is good
enough for her.   I shall ever have the most
affectionate regard for my old playfellow, to whom
I hope some day to present my own sweet Mary.'
I could see she was deeply moved, and the letter,
which was pressed in her fingers, fell to the
ground.   With averted face she held her hand to
me, and said—' Dear Doctor, it is late; I must get
back.   Good night,' as she passed out into the
hall.   In another moment I heard a heavy fall.
She had fainted—my poor girl!   But why am I
dwelling on these things?   She is among the
angels in heaven, far from all care and sorrow.
Dick Butler was as good a husband to her as it was
in his nature to be; but when she died, after little
Mary's birth, he went, as you and I know, Bates,
to the deuce at the rate of a hunt.   Presently I
began to hear news from India I did not like at all.
Your father had scarcely ever cost me a penny; but
now bills began to come in with excuses about the expenses of house-furnishing and housekeeping.   He
had to keep an establishment—his wife had been accustomed to live in great style, and all the rest of it.
There were accounts of his splendid entertainments,

and of his wife's balls, and parties, and jewels—of her horses and plate—and poor Lough-na-Carra began to feel it; and the bills became larger instead of smaller, and came oftener, until at last—my God! —I dreaded the mails. There was a change in his letters I did not like: he was either reckless or gloomy—he began to admit there were some little motes in his sunbeam—that she really was careless of money, and too fond of pleasure and admiration. 'But,' he added, ' she is a mere child; and really, if I could take her to England to-morrow I would put her to school, if I could, only for a certain event which is coming off, and which makes me a little anxious about her. These Indian-reared girls are spoiled by native nurses, and when a girl is so very remarkable as Mary for her loveliness, she is apt to get a liking for admiration, and to make a jealous, proud fellow like me rather unreasonable and sulky now and then.' I see you growing pale, my dear Terry; but it is best, as I have begun, that you should know all. Bates, give him a glass of wine; it will do him good, and enable him to get through my story. Our correspondence became at last not what it ought to be between father and son. All my hopes and plans for the future—for his sake, mind—were shattered, and at last I was obliged to write out that I could stand his demands no longer—that I could afford still to let him have £300 a-year, and the money for his majority, if he wanted the latter; but that would leave nothing for improvements, and but little for myself."

" Faith, and that's true," interrupted Mr. Bates; " and the captain ought to have known it well enough."

" Ah, well! Bates, we must not be too hard on him. Remember whom he had to deal with, and how completely he was her slave. I confess, when he wrote to ask me whether I could not manage to send him his allowance for ten years in a lump, as well as his majority—after I had paid very nearly £4000 for him in the previous year or so—I lost my temper. I refused point blank; angry letters—some from him quite in-coherent—passed, and at last a sullen silence, which was finally broken in tears by the news of his death." The old man paused, and after a moment went on, " You were born shortly before that. In those days letters took months to travel between here and India; and when I heard you were born my heart was softened, and our good friend there raised some money, and I sent it out to your father; but it arrived too late for any good purpose, and was spent as so much before it had been. The only comfort I had was, that just before the news of his death I received a few lines, in a broken, shaking hand, to make his peace; and I little imagined they were to be his last, and that they were written from his dying bed. In them he said, indeed, that he longed to get away home, and that his health had suffered a little; but he feared he could not arrange with the banks to leave India; 'and if,' added he, 'I should be carried off here, it is a consolation to think you will look after my widow and the dear little fellow. Mary will need some one with a very resolute temper to deal with her. She cannot understand we are not all as rich as some of her native nabobs and rajahs, or as some foolish young officers appear to be, because they run riot and get smashed in a few years; and it will do her good to see how English ladies bring up their families.' Ah, my boy, it is a sad story, and it grows sadder still." He paused again, and looked at Mr. Bates, who sat silent at the table, with one hand across his brow, in the gathering shades of the summer evening. "You perceive, Terry, I knew nothing of your mother—nothing except what the picture he sent us told; and when it came home with your father's, it was easy to comprehend how such a face had led the dear fellow to forget everything else.   Then came the intelligence of his death."——

My grandfather ceased, and the tears trickled down his cheek beneath his thin hand.   There was silence for a time, then he continued.   " The last news I had was from your father's agent to say that he had secured a passage for your mother, and her infant (yourself), and her servants, and that he had drawn upon me for £300 to cover the expenses ; that his effects, such as they were, would be sold, but that there were many claims, which it would need a large sum of money to meet, of which he would send particulars in due course. I will not trouble you with all that part of a subject, which is quite pain- ful enough as it is.   God knows how I watched the days as the time drew near when I might expect your mother and her little one.   It is now nearly twelve years since that time.   At last you came, but not your mother——"

" Ah, I know, she was drowned—my poor darling mother !" I interrupted.

" Don't distress me, Terry.   It is hard enough as it is.   Oh, Bates ! how am I to go on ?   Well, well, it must be done.   Terry, take that letter and read it, and heaven comfort you, my dear, dear boy."

The old man raised his hands and covered his face, leaning his elbows on the table.

The letter he gave me was, as I have said, discoloured and yellow, and the ink was pale, but the writing was so bold and sharp that when I went to the window I could read it without difficulty. It ran thus :—

"The *Ross-shire* Indiaman, at sea, May 18th.

" MY DEAR FATHER-IN-LAW,—You have been prepared for the intelligence of poor dear Jack's death, and how I and my child are coming to live with you, as he desired. Since I came on board I have been very sick, but I am now better. We have got very nice people on board. Jack left me very badly off; and I have been obliged to borrow, oh, ever so much rupees; but that is of no matter. What I am thinking of is seriously that I ought not to have come away at all. You know my marriage was a very unfortunate one for me. I could have had the best possible matches ; but I loved your son so much I did not mind anything; and being young and inexperienced, I never could have supposed he would have proposed for me unless he was quite able to keep up a good establishment. It turned out he was quite poor; and oh, you cannot imagine how

I have suffered ! And latterly, when he took to drinking too much brandy pawnee, and grumbled dreadfully, my life was miserable; and I was afraid to speak to any one lest he should quarrel with him. You see, I tell you everything, although I have seen such cross letters of yours to him when he only asked for money that was really wanted. My son Terence is a very pretty little fellow, but the ayah tells me he has quite a shocking temper; and though I whip him a good deal he gets more violent, and I am obliged to keep away from him, not to get cross and fret myself. And now, dear Doctor Brady, what I am coming to is this: I am sure I shall not like Ireland or England. My health already suffers, for I am very delicate and dreadfully sensitive. Well, then, why should you not allow me, say, rupees 600 a month, and take my dear little son, and educate him until he grows up? I would stay in India somewhere. I have plenty of friends; and Captain Fraser, who is coming down to Madras, says he can get me very nicely introduced among his friends and some nice people at Hyderabad. I think I shall leave the ship at Galle, in Ceylon, where we are going to touch, and send on little Terry and his own servants to you till I know what you think. I am an odd kind of creature, and would upset your house very much; but if you wish to have me home for a time, of course I shall go to you; and perhaps it may be necessary for me to do so, in order to sign papers and things to secure my annuity. I am told you must have lawyers to make what I propose quite legal and binding on your property, though Captain Fraser says the best way is to pay the whole into bank at once. I shall be eighteen in two months; and any of the insurance offices can calculate, he says, what £700 a-year would be worth at that time of life. Under all the circumstances, I think it will be best for me to forfeit the passage-money and land at Madras or Galle till I hear from you. My address will be to the care of Colville and Arbuthnot, Madras, as I do not want Macknight, my husband's agent, who is a very troublesome sort of man, to carry on my business. You must excuse so many shakes in my hand, as the ship is not quite steady at times. I should like Terry, I think, to go into the army when he grows up. His great relations abroad would get him on.

" Hoping yet to have the pleasure of seeing you, I beg you to believe me,

" Your most affectionate daughter,
" MARY BRADY.

" Postscriptum.—Jack always promised me a set of diamond and pearl court ornaments which you have belonging to his dear mother. They will reach me safely if sent to Colville and Arbuthnot, Madras, through their agents of the same name in Hart-lane, City of London. By this mail you will receive a good many bills and accounts which my poor dear husband could not settle; and I shall have, if I stay at Madras or Galle, to write an order on you for a few thousand rupees, just to pay expenses. Mohun has some things for you, and my pet monkey. Please make Terry always remember he is a gentleman ; for I am told that Ireland is a very odd sort of place. Poor Jack was quite an exception to the people there generally, I am told. But he had his faults.—M.B."

I read the letter with the intensest interest, little heeding the low whistles and phews which came at intervals from Mr. Bates, or the drumming of my grandfather's fingers on the table ; and then I looked up and said, " Poor mamma was drowned after she wrote this. You see, grandpapa, how fond she was of me. I am almost the last person she speaks of, except papa."

My grandfather raised his head and looked at me

with a curious stare. He then gazed across the table
at Mr. Bates, who only filled his glass again, and said
softly, " Good lad ! good lad ! Why shouldn't he
say so ?"

My grandfather stretched out his hand, took up
the letter, and returned it to the bundle. Selecting
another letter from those which lay before him,
still with the same expression on his face, he said,
" Terry, read this next."

It was dated " Madras, May 23rd."

" MY DEAREST FATHER-IN-LAW,—Since I wrote to
you I have been thinking more and more of what
I said, and I have made up my mind not to go to
Europe. I am sure you will see I am right, and
that you will make the provision I propose for your
dear son's poor unfortunate widow. I can live very
well here in the way I am accustomed to at what
Captain Fraser tells me would not be enough to
have even the ordinary necessaries of life in Europe.
The little boy will not miss me. When he grows
up, of course he will come out here; and if you
could get him into poor dear Jack's regiment I
could look after him. As there are a number of
ladies on board, I am not going to tell any one when
I go on shore to-night. They are all spiteful old

things, full of ' gup,' as we say, or scandal; and I
am going to play them a trick which will amuse
you. There is a sergeant's wife who is a steerage
passenger, and it is arranged she is to come to my
cabin and take my place till the trick is discovered.
I have not been on deck more than once or twice,
and a little money goes a long way with these sort
of people, so that not a word will be said. I ought
not to disguise from you that Captain Fraser wishes,
when a proper time has passed, to make me his
wife, provided that you carry out my proposal, as
no doubt you will. It is the best thing I could do.
He has already lent me money, which I told you I
wanted. To prevent any mischief from the tongues
of the idle creatures who are jealous of my good
looks, Captain Fraser will go on to Galle, and will
visit Mrs. Lynnett, the sergeant's wife, in my cabin,
as if it was I; but he is to come back to Madras as
soon as possible; and if I am not quite comfortable there, I shall go to Hyderabad, where he has a
sister married. My only pang is parting with my
son, and not seeing you. But we will all three
meet some time. The ship is off Madras in the
roads; I must get ready for my plot. All the servants are delighted, as I shall let them come in
different boats on shore, and only the ayah, Meetum,

and Mohun, will go on with Terry. Mohun is to stay and watch Terry. Send out the money, or as much as you can, at once.

" Your affectionate daughter,

" With a thousand kisses,

" MARY BRADY.

" P.S.—I am very anxious to hear from you. Be sure you let me know how Terry looks when he arrives. I can wear the diamonds and pearls in mourning out here; so it will be as well to let me have them soon."

I followed every word as closely as I could; but it was impossible to understand it. A hundred different thoughts flew through my head in a moment. My eyes rested on the letter without noting the words; but somehow or other there was rising up in my mind the image of a frivolous, mercenary woman, who was about to abandon her child, and who was already contemplating—whilst her husband, of whom she had written so slightingly, was scarcely cold in his grave—a marriage with a stranger. Could this be the mother whose image had been to me scarcely less sacred than——I could not dwell on the thought. There was silence in the room; the two old men sat in the shade at the table, whilst I stood at the window to catch the light just vanishing into darkness. " Then, grandpapa, where was it mamma was drowned? and what is the meaning of all this? I have looked at the map over and over again, and I can't understand it. My mother was wrecked after this, wasn't she ?"

My grandfather got up from his chair and came to my side ; he put his hand on my shoulder and said in a low voice, " I would have kept you ignorant of the truth, which is known to very few of us here. It is no wonder you cannot see into such a dark story. Your mother, my dear boy—grieved am I to say it—was not worthy of your father, and is not worthy of your love. Do not start or shrink from the truth. They say she is naturally very clever; but in these letters there is as much folly as heartlessness. She ruined your father, and in his ruin involved me and you, my poor fellow. Now, do you not see that it was not your mother who was swept away by that wave when the *Ross-shire's* decks were deluged by the sea ?"   .

" And where, then, is my mother?" I cried. " What became of her? Why did she not come home to us?"

" Your tears distress me, Terry. Why fix your

thoughts on one who never cared for you, or showed the smallest particle of affection? Your mother left Calcutta with the deliberate intention of abandoning you for ever. She fled to escape her creditors, and, as it seems, too plainly—you must know how your grandfather, who loves you, feels as he tells you this—with the purpose of flying with one who was her lover ere she married your father—a needy, dissolute man. She managed to get on shore at Madras unobserved—your mother could pass, I am told, for a native woman anywhere, and was an adept in disguises; her greatest talent, indeed, was displayed on the stage, and in private theatricals she made the most startling impression. At all events, she went on shore at Madras, as I have said, and then came the gale at sea which drove the ship out of her course, so that she struck on the rocks and was all but lost. The poor woman who took her place was among those who perished as she rushed out of the cabin. There was great confusion on board; and when the *Ross-shire*, in a sinking state, got into Galle harbour, the passengers left her, and not much notice was taken of the fate of the poor sergeant's wife, whilst every one spoke of your mother's melancholy death. It was best to let it be thought so. Surely the Providence of God works marvels to our eyes!   I cannot but feel, however, there is a compensation to all our grief in the escape you have had from the influence of such a woman.   I do not ask you to restrain your sorrows.   I know how rudely the tendrils of your young heart must be torn by the tale I have to tell, and how fondly you cherished the memory of that unfortunate woman; but you will cease to regret or to think of her; you must banish so unworthy a mother and wife from your thoughts, or think of her as one who is indeed lost to you—lost in a death of shame.   A thousand times better had it been for her and you and us all had she been borne to her grave beneath the waters, than live to work mischief and revel in her deceit and guilt. These are hard words, my son; but they are gentle words for her conduct to me and mine—to the name she bore.   Again I say, Terry, banish her from your thoughts.   She has wrought misery and sorrow enough in our house; but now it would seem as if she had vanished, or as if she has sunk into some depth where our eyes had best not strive to follow her."

"She is still alive?" I asked—the word "mother" could not now be formed by my lips; I felt cold and sick at heart—"she is still alive somewhere in

the world ? You cannot now refuse to tell me !
Where is she now ?—oh ! where ?"

" The last news I heard of the woman was, that
she was living at the court of one of the native
princes in India, still beautiful, and still busy in
intrigue and mischief. Unhappy creature ! She
has passed through a world of adventure, and has
been traced under a variety of names ; but in her
letters to me she has always persisted in claiming
our name."

" But if she married Captain Fraser, why does
she not call herself after his name ?"

" Alas, my dear Terry, you probe too deeply for
your own peace. Captain Fraser, as I told you,
was needy and dissolute. He was well connected—
by marriage a cousin of the Desmonds, and by blood
allied with some of the great Scotch families which
rule in India. Well, when he found that I would
not accede to the modest request of my daughter-
in-law, he thought perhaps that it would be a useless and dangerous experiment to marry so extravagant a woman. At all events, he married a very
plain, delicate—but, as I have heard, very amiable—
girl, who came out to India to her father, a great
civilian, and who had a large fortune."

" By-the-by, I hear that Mr. Desmond has taken

their daughter to live with him," interrupted Mr. Bates. "Where is Colonel Fraser since the row?"

" He is somewhere in what they call the Deccan, I hear. When Malcolm died all his money went to Mrs. Fraser; after her death it was found Fraser could not touch a penny of it, for every farthing was settled on her daughter most rigidly, and then went away to distant relations, except a considerable sum to his friend Desmond."

" Miss Fraser will be well off, Doctor," observed Mr. Bates; " only for Mary Butler, Desmond would adopt her; if Sir Richard does not marry, she might own the Castle estates, and Kilmoyle, instead of poor Mary. And then, Doctor, who knows? She might take a fancy to Terry, and the land would go back into the old hands."

" It is a charming fancy sketch, Bates. You are better fitted to be a poet than an attorney. I have too many realities, and sad ones, to indulge in any dreams of the future with the least ray of light in them."

" Oh, sir, if you knew how dark my future looks too," I sobbed. " My dreams are gone indeed. But I tell you, grandfather, that I will never be satisfied till I see her face to face, and let her explain what has passed."

" See her !" exclaimed the old man, almost angrily; " see her after what you have heard ! Why, only I thought it would be needless, I was about to ask you to promise me solemnly, if at any future time of your life you should be near her, to shun that woman as you would the Evil One."

" She is my mother, sir," I interrupted.

" But I tell you, Terence, she is as dangerous as she is bad. Do you know that, far distant as she is from us, for years she was plotting against you, or rather I believed she was, whereas her real object was to extort money from me by working on my fears. She declared she would come over and claim her child—that she had witnesses to prove all the stories I had heard of her were false—that her husband's last will and his last words were, that she was to have charge of you ; and she raked up all kinds of accusations against the dead man's memory, which at least she would have dragged before the public. She employed Mohun as her spy in my house, and had minute accounts of everything which passed till I sent him away. I am now quite satisfied," he continued, angrily, " that some of the large sums I paid after your father's death were on forgeries, for in addition to her arts of imitation, she can copy handwriting so as to defy all but the minutest inspection.   Terence," he exclaimed, passionately, " if you ever speak to her—should you, as is most unlikely, ever meet—you will disobey my last injunction to you, and you will dishonour your father's memory."

The servant bringing in lights silenced me as I was about to fly into a wild, passionate vindication.   I could only sob in silence.

We sat at table, and my grandfather, after a pause, continued—

" You know well enough I would not advise you to do anything unbecoming a son.   When you are a little older, and can understand what she has done clearly, you will feel my advice is right.   But it is not likely you will ever see her.   You will all your life, however, have to endure the consequences of her acts.   All the efforts I was making to clear off the encumbrances from my poor estate for my son, and you after him, have been made of no avail, and we are more deeply in debt than ever.   One of her constant threats was that she would get you carried away from me; and she actually took steps to frighten me into the belief she was in earnest. You remember, Bates, my writing to you about the two fellows who stopped at the ' Desmond Arms' one night, and made so many inquiries after Terry's movements, and who came from Galway and went back there ?"

" Faith, I do, Doctor; but I told you if it meant anything at all it was to screw some more money out of you. Terry would have made a large bundle for them to carry off, and I wouldn't give much for their lives if you raised the county on them. I daresay you would have made a fight, and used your voice if not your fists, Terry ?"

" Perhaps you were right, Bates ; but anyway, I confess I have a terror of the woman with whom I battled in secret for so many years. She was quite capable of getting an injury done to him to injure me and to have her revenge. It was my fear of something of the kind made me send him to school, for there I knew he would be less accessible—he would have boys always around him. Ah ! Bates, my heart sank within me when I got Dr. Ball's letter telling me of the terrible cruise. I cannot feel he is safe when he is out of my sight even now. I am full of vague, nervous fears; all I pray is to live till he is able to protect himself."

" Well, Doctor, it seems as if he was pretty near that stage already. I will bid you good night now. It is quite obvious you have done what is right. Keep what you have heard to yourself my young friend—there is no use in telling all the world ; and I believe, for the matter of that, a good many people have suspicions about that drowning, and that in India, at all events, there is a good part of the story known.   But people wont bother their heads about it.   It's not the boy's fault, and these things are soon forgotten.   Good night ; we will have another look into these serious affairs to-morrow and see what can be done.   I must take the night mail to Dublin ; but I hope we can strike out some way of arranging matters for you, my dear old friend."

CHAPTER X.

When Mr. Bates withdrew, my grandfather remained deep in thought for a moment, and then called me over to him.

"You see in this desk, Terence, are all the letters relating to yourself, your poor father, and her of whom we have now been speaking—in fact, all that relates to your sad story, to her exactions and frauds, and to the money that has been torn from me. They are in this secret drawer—it closes so; put your finger there and press. See, it opens ! Here, again, are documents and deeds connected with the property, such as it is. Bates has the leases and all that kind of thing. This is a duplicate key, and I give it to you to keep. Never let it leave your possession. You can when you are old enough examine the papers in my desk, and read and think for yourself. So now take it back to the

15—2

study, and ring the bell for the servants. You must read prayers for them to-night, as I am tired and want to go to bed; but come in and bid me good night as usual."

It was ten o'clock, and the bell rang for prayers. Only two of the servants were Protestants; but an old crone who, long past her work, spent her days by the kitchen fire, and slept in the gardener's house, named Biddy Daly, was accustomed to accompany them to the parlour in order to give vent to her groans and moans, and to have a look at the " young masther," as she termed my grandfather, and " Masther Jack's child," and to make a formal statement on the subject of her rheumatiz to the Doctor —indeed, she was wont to waylay him at all hours, and in unexpected places for that purpose, and no menaces or repression shook her intrepidity of soul or her courage in communicating the latest information concerning her bodily health, under all circumstances and at all times. Even the interference of the priest, which was brought to bear in a friendly manner by a little intrigue between him and his old friend, did not deter Biddy from the " parlour prayers for the Protesdans," as she called them.

" It's not to listen to their prayers, poor craychers—the Virgin between us and harm!—your reverence, I goes; but shure, whin I'm racked wid the pains I've got in sarvin' the family, the laste the young masther can do is to ordher poor ould Biddy some stuff. I always take some holy wather in wid me for fear of the divil, and ses me own Pather and Avey afore I go to bed—indeed I do, your reverence."

When Biddy saw me sitting with the Prayer-book before me, and that the Doctor had retired, she expressed her feeling of displeasure very audibly, and lamenting, with several ochones, that " I nivir can see the young masther, and me worse than iver to-night—me bottle of stuff all tuk, too. It's little good yer prayers 'll do me this night," crawled out of the room again.

I read the service for my little congregation, and taking up my candle whilst the servants were fastening up doors and windows, went softly to the room in which hung the picture I had regarded with such indescribable affection till that moment. The apartment was in darkness, but by holding the candle over my head I caught the face, whilst the greater part of the painting was but partly visible. How lovely! how innocent! how pure! I had ever deemed it before. But now, as I looked, the eyes, in their cold dreaminess, had a glitter like that which filled the orbs of the tiger-cat with which she was playing—the lips seemed bitter and cruel—and the attitude in which she was lying, her dress, and all the luxurious accessories of the painting, belonged, in my mind, to a frivolous, extravagant woman, heartless as the wall against which it rested. There was a positive fascination in the steady, sleepy smile of the eyes, and lowering my candle, with a shudder I mounted the stairs to my grandfather's bed-room. He was in bed, apparently reading by the light of his lamp, the curtains drawn on the side next the door, so that he did not perceive my entrance or hear my footsteps. A large Bible was open on his reading-stand ; but I observed that his eyes were half closed, as if he were engaged in thought, and that his lips were moving, as though he were speaking to himself. At last he opened his eyes, and seeing me, said, with his usual smile—

"Ah! there you are, Terry. Come to bid me good night. It's nearly time, or you will lose your beauty sleep. Well, and how did you get on? I wish you had prescribed for old Biddy in place of me. She actually crept upstairs here, and only I threatened her with the watch-stand as she put her head through the curtains, the old nuisance would have commenced her litany as usual."

" Biddy came into the parlour, but she vanished when she saw you were not there, and I thought she went down the kitchen stairs."

" I really must have her brought to her senses, if she has any. Do you know, Terry, I have been having most curious waking dreams: talking so much of a certain subject has filled my poor old brain full of fancies, and as soon as I had banished old Biddy, others took her place."

" Others ! What do you mean, grandfather ?"

" Well, I can scarcely say, in my half-dozing state. The curtain appeared to open, and a face like that—you know—below stairs looked in at me ; but, of course, when I roused myself it was gone. The idea was not pleasant, for the look of the lady-visitor was not at all amiable. All this means, Terry, an excited nervous system, and a good deal of indigestion, and you shall hand me over that medicine chest and give me one of my famous ' composers' before you go."

I had walked towards the escritoire in which the chest was, when my attention was attracted by an exclamation from my grandfather, and a whispered cry. " Terry, look !—look ! there it is again."

As I turned towards the bed the curtains were just closing, as if some one who had drawn them aside let them go ! But I had a glimpse of something like a face, and a pair of hands clasped together, inside the bed ere the folds met together.   Never doubting that it was old Biddy who had come to persecute " the masther," as she had been very troublesome lately, and regarded his illness as a personal wrong to herself rather than to him, I took up my candle and sprang swiftly round the bed.   There was no one in the room ! The door was slightly ajar ; I went out on the landing, peered over the banisters—not a creature visible. The voice of my grandfather called me back. " Well, and have you caught the culprit ?" he asked. " Give her a good shaking and have her locked up in her room to-night."

" But Biddy's not there. She's not on the stairs or anywhere I could see."

" You saw the old woman yourself, didn't you ?"

" I saw somebody, certainly, as if the curtains had been opened and let fall again. It must be Biddy."

My grandfather seemed a little agitated.

" Go down," said he, " and see if the servants are all in bed. Tell the cook to look if Biddy is in her room."

I did as I was directed, and in a few minutes returned with a paler face, to say—" Old Biddy was fast asleep in bed, where she has been, they say, for the last hour; and not one of the servants has been upstairs."

" Then the only thing I can think of, Terry," he replied, with a faint smile, " is that we have both seen the Banshee. I believe there is a lady of that description who does this branch of the family the honour of attending on them when *in periculo*. At all events, I shall take my composer; and you, my dear boy, will, I hope, sleep away all your troubles and cares under the protection of Him who will shield you from all danger, as long as you seek His grace and protection."

I went over to the escritoire, took the medicine-chest, and was coming back with it towards the table—my grandfather had turned round in bed to screen the light from his eyes—the lamp shone full on the folds of the heavy grey curtains between me and the door—I was as collected and as sensible as I am now when, with pen in hand, in the light of day, and in possession of my senses, I record what happened.

The curtain opened a little way—two thin

white arms and hands, with interlaced fingers, were lifted up over the bed through the opening, and I saw a pale face, with fair or white hair falling over the shoulders, bent down as if the eyes were fixed on the old man. The hands unlocked thrice, and were clasped together again with a slow waving motion, as if in sorrow or distress, and then the apparition vanished! Not a word came from my grandfather's lips. I stood rooted to the spot. The appearance was so sudden, that ere I could do more than utter a smothered ejaculation of terror, it was gone! The cry aroused my grandfather, who had been lying with closed eyes, and he looked round and asked, " What is the matter now, Terry?" With more presence of mind and self-control than I had thought myself capable of exerting, I said, " Oh, nothing, sir. I nearly let the case fall ;" and indeed my hands were shaking as if with an ague fit.

Putting down the case on the table, I ran swiftly towards the door, candle in hand, looked over the banisters, into the hall, up and down the corridor, behind the big clock, examined all the doors on the landing, and was back almost ere the curtains had ceased to vibrate.

To no eye but mine had the figure been visible ; or

at least, if my grandfather saw it, he kept his own counsel. But he said very calmly, "It is time for you to go to bed indeed. There; now let us see what my composer will do. I have strange fancies in my head, and am haunted by that wretched old Biddy, who has set one of her kindred witches to persecute me."

I kissed the old man's brow, turned down his lamp, and fled along the passage to my own room, locked the door, and throwing myself on my knees, implored the mercy and protection of heaven. My pulse was beating wildly, and I almost cried aloud with terror as I rose from my knees, for the copy of " the" picture above my little bed seemed to move, and the face, to my disordered senses, assumed an expression of animation, and a smile of derision curled the opening lips. I gazed at the canvas steadily, and perceived that I was distracted by imaginary terrors; but somehow or other I could not bear the thought that these eyes would be on me at night staring in the leaden look which the copyist had conveyed to them, and so I got up, and with great difficulty unhooked the frame and turned the face to the wall. I was a great strong lad; I had no superstitious fears, no morbid fancies, except those which were connected with my brooding over the absent mother I had indeed lost at last ; but somehow or other there was upon me a terror—a secret horror, indescribable, profound—at what I had seen. Was I awake? Could I doubt the evidence of my senses? Had not my grandfather seen it too? But he was weak, nervous, and excited. Was I quite sure I was not led away by my own vivid fancy to believe in the repetition of a sick man's dream? I could not bear to blow out the light; and as it flickered in the currents of air which sympathized with the rising storm, the shadows on the wall begat new terrors. My head was throbbing; I heard the beatings of my own heart as though some one was thumping the pillow on which I lay. The muttering of the thunder and the flashes of lightning which now flitted through the shutters were a welcome distraction. As the storm rolled towards the house, and the rain beat against the glass, I felt more at ease. But sleep would not visit my eyelids. There came on me a lethargy, in which I dreamt as I lay awake. It seemed as if I could look out into the corridor through wall and door, and that I could see where my grandfather lay asleep. His slumbers were agitated : his hands played about with the coverlet, and his arms were now and then lifted in the air as he tossed on his uneasy bed. Suddenly I beheld, growing out of the shadow of the door of his room, which was opened by an invisible hand, a shape which waved like a vapour in the faint light of the night-lamp. It gathered form and substance as I gazed—a woman's face, of ghastly pallor, peering with weeping eyes through masses of white hair, and outstretched arms raised as if in anguish. A crashing peal of thunder shook the house, a cry of agony, which pierced the deep roar of the angry heavens, came from the corridor! In a second I was awake. I had thrown off the nightmare, and unlocked my door and rushed out into the passage with the candle in my hand. Mr. Bates, in his nightshirt, was standing at his bedroom door with a light in the current.

"Did you hear a scream, Terry—did you cry out just at the last clap of thunder?"

"Oh, sir, I'm so glad you are awake. Come to grandfather's room. I fear something has happened."

For all my agitation, it did not escape me that the door which I had shut as I came away was now half open.

In a moment all was told. My grandfather was lying as if he had been trying to rise, and had fallen back on his pillow! I had never seen

death yet; but as I gazed on the face before
me, I knew the Conqueror had been there. The
old man's eyes were open, looking straight into
space; his jaw had fallen, and a little stream
of blood trickled slowly from his lip upon the
pillow; the hand of one arm was clenched as if
in anger across his heart, the other still held the
curtain in its gripe.

CHAPTER XI.

OUT ON THE WORLD.

Oh, how I welcomed the day as its first streaks
lighted the waters of the lake! The night was too
full of terrors. Mr. Bates sat beside me in the
parlour, trying to comfort me. There was no
sound in the house, save the creaking of the boards
as the servants busied themselves in arranging the
room in which the dead man lay. Dr. Brophy had
already seen him; there could be no doubt of the
cause of death. Apoplexy had stricken the old man,
" caused," said the doctor, " probably by undue exertion before he was recovered from his last serious attack." When the servants were summoned by Mr.
Bates and myself, they all concurred in stating they
heard a loud cry—" yell," the housekeeper said—
just as the last great peal of thunder made the rooms
quiver; indeed, they were nearly all awake, and
the maids were cowering together in their room

at the time.   Old Biddy, whom I sent one of them to look for, was found fast asleep in spite of her ailments; and the gardener declared " she was snorin' as if she was strivin' to bate the thunder."

I told Mr. Bates what I had seen.   He shook his head, and said, " My boy, you have gone through too much; I must get the doctor to have a look at you.   See here, Terry; your grand-father's old and faithful servant will take charge of the house, and see everything done that is neces-sary.   I will take on myself to give the orders needed; but I must go to Dublin to-night.   You can do no good fretting and moping here; and as I know I am one of your guardians, I must begin to use my power.   Nay, my boy, I will not, if you desire indeed to stay.   But I advise you to come with me, and we will return together when the proper time comes."

After a little I gave way and consented to leave Lough-na-Carra.   I gave my last embrace to him I loved so well.   A thousand memories of his tender affection—of his kindness to me—his care and soli-citude—his anxiety—of his disappointments and suf-fering—crowded upon me, and with agonized sob-bings I pressed my lips to the cold cheek, and addressed passionate entreaties for forgiveness for all my offences to the ear which could never hear again till the dead awake to judgment.

It was all over. As chief mourner I had followed the remains of my only friend to the grave. It was, after the Irish fashion, " a great funeral." All the neighbouring gentry came or sent their carriages; squires, farmers, peasants trooped to the church; the Roman Catholic bishop of the diocese attended the cortège to the gates, in company with the priests of the district; and when it was done and I sat in my room, " breaking my heart," as Honour declared, the noise of chinking plates and glasses, and the sounds which came up from the hall and large dining-room, where breakfast was laid out for all who chose to partake of it, appeared to be a mockery of what we had just heard from the reverend rector, whose voice was audible below, delivering an *éloge* on the deceased.

Those were weary days during which I struggled with fresh sorrow as every familiar object recalled the good old man. Mr. Bates remained with me, looking over papers, burning letters, examining accounts, paying bills, seeing creditors and land agents, solicitors and local attorneys. The house and servants smelt of fresh crape, and even the summer sun could not dispel the gloom which haunted every chamber. Mr. Bates grew more grave and anxious as he proceeded with his work of investigation.

" It is a terrible muddle. But I can make out well enough there will not be much for you; and I doubt if we can save even Lough-na-Carra. You are heir to everything he had, and, except some legacies to servants, and souvenirs to a few friends, your grandfather leaves, in trust till you are twenty-one years old, all he possessed. But it is terribly mortgaged and encumbered, and the tenants have played the deuce lately. He was always too easy with the fellows. Sir Philip has renounced his trust, as he has too much to do; Sir Richard is too careless to be of much use—and, indeed, I wonder why my old friend put him in ; and I suppose I shall have to do the best I can for you. Just see what odd things happen ; of course I don't pay the least attention to their impertinence."

I took the letter which my guardian handed to me. It was addressed—" To the Executors of Myles Brady, Esquire, M.D., Lough-na-Carra, Kilmoyle, Ireland," and ran as follows :—

"20th June, 18—.
"Chancery Lane, London.

"GENTLEMEN,—Noticing the death of Myles Brady, Esq., M.D., of Lough-na-Carra, we beg to inform you that, as attorneys for Mary Brady, widow of the late Captain John Brady, of her Majesty's —th Regiment of Infantry, and mother of Terence Brady, minor, it is our client's intention to take immediate steps to assume the guardianship of her son, which belongs to her by law; and also to enforce from the trustees of the estate of the late Dr. Brady, in addition to such sum as the Court may order for her son's education and maintenance, repayment of various sums, amounting in all to Rs. 73,607 and 4 annas, with interest at 5 per cent., due from the deceased to her late husband. Whilst Dr. Brady lived, our client, from various motives of a highly honourable and disinterested character, refrained from doing more than establishing the validity of her claims; and writing under correction of advices to be received from India, we may remark that an immediate settlement might induce her to accept a portion of her debt in lieu of the whole, and at the same time resign her to the possibility of leaving her son in charge of those to whom Dr. Brady may have made him over.

"Your obedient servants,

"McTurk & Skinner."

"The scoundrels!" ejaculated Mr. Bates. "They don't know whom they have got to deal with here. These are fellows who speculate in Indian cases, and are allied with a set of greater rascals, if possible, out in Bombay. They are at the bottom of half the appeals to the Privy Council, and are on the look-out for claims all over the world to keep their dirty trade going. Can they suppose we don't know poor Jack Brady was insolvent, or that we are ignorant of what a nice lady their client is? Dash their impudence! Let them try it, that's all."

It was resolved to let Lough-na-Carra, as soon as it could be made out what there was to let; to sell part of the estate; and then to see what could be done with me. My natural inclination led me to enter the army; but Mr. Bates was not so much enamoured of the profession of arms as most Irishmen, even of his class, are. He began to doubt if the rent of Lough-na-Carra and the sale of the best part of the property would do more than pay off some incumbrances and provide for the interest of mortgages, leaving a very small pittance for my education; and he argued that if money were to be raised for my commission and to lodge for purchase of steps, it would sink the little property altogether, and leave me little or nothing beyond my pay to live on—and that's "easier," said he, "to talk about than to do."

Sir Richard Desmond's only interference was on that point—" The lad, after all, is a gentleman, and what else can he do but carry a sword? The law. is a beggarly profession—I beg your pardon, Bates, for you belong to the branch of it which is never raised to the peerage, and is always making money. The boy is not made for the Church, and there's not a living for him to be brought up to. Doctors are respectable, and they are lucky in Ireland, where they are made knights and baronets, and make fortunes, and have banished general practitioners among the poorest community in Europe; but I don't see my way to the boy's becoming a model medico, either surgeon or doctor."

But Sir Richard was a languid, easy man : when he stated his case he did not care about fighting it. For myself, provided I could not go into the army, I did not care much what career in life was selected for me; but I had positively made up my mind to bend the course of any pursuit in which I might be engaged towards India. There was a hand pointing to that land of mystery, whichever way I turned—a secret sympathy which called me from afar, and whispered that there was some purpose of my life to be served which it would be well to carry out quickly. There was much work to be done with the lawyers, and meantime it was proposed I should return to Dr. Ball's; but I felt I could do more good at a school where there was less Latin and Greek, where I would have complete change of scene. Sir Richard suggested "Eton" or "Harrow;" Mr. Bates said—"No! we've got no money. I don't so much say for the charges, though Eton would be high enough, but for the tastes and incidental expenses. Besides, Terry, with his brogue and his ways, would be in misery among them, and would get into no end of rows with his hot blood, in which he would most likely get licked, until he learned some pugilistic tricks from his opponents."

Sir Richard, for once, persisted in his opinion. " I am for an English school; I don't say for a girl, though women are cosmopolitan. But from what I remember of my youth, I have no great faith in the British boarding-school. I can't fancy a worse training for a young girl than to be at your fashionable watering-place, and to see the full tide of fashion, frivolity, and vice flowing under her eyes, as if it were the ocean of life itself. Boys must be men, and there is no use in stamping on them early in life a brand which marks them with a distinction which is very like a certificate of inferiority. We must submit to lose our nationality in the imperial vortex, or be treated as provincials."

CHAPTER XII.

As a compromise, it was resolved I should be sent to the great Preparatory College of Sweatenham; and Mr. Bates and myself were soon afterwards on our way to the pleasant town on which the founders of the seminary had pitched as a good place to feather the nests of its principal and masters.

When the packet ran alongside the dock quay at Liverpool, I was surprised to see a swarming, ragged crowd, the counterpart of that which I had left behind me, save that they were sulky instead of being good-humoured, scrambling for the luggage of the passengers, for I had been taught to regard dirt and poverty as exclusively Irish. But, as Mr. Bates said, "If they're not Irish, they're Welsh—cousin-germans, if not brothers—hating each other in a brotherly fashion, at all events."

The smoke of the grimy city, its squalor and its

misery, the yellow Mersey groaning beneath its burden of keels, the forest of masts rising above the dock walls like the trees in some garden where gold and silver are planted and cropped—the bustle in the streets, the vast bales of cotton towering in gigantic vans, and the long piles of sombre warehouses hauling up and letting down merchandize from their lean arm-like cranes—all astonished rather than pleased me.

Forth from the dock, slow warping to the stream, came the bow of a great ship, with her white sails gracefully festooned from the yards, and her lofty spars shining like polished metal; a huge ensign flew from her gaff, displaying its pale stars and bright blue ground, and broad flakes of red on the white cloth. The crew, manning the capstan with a " stamp and go" to the sound of a fiddle, shouted in chorus as the Magnus Apollo of the band closed each stanza of his song, and the spanker flapped in the breeze like thunder. But above all the tumult and din came that bitter sobbing, the echoes of the fountain of sorrow and despair flooding from the heart, which can only be heard as one listens to the farewell of the Irish emigrant ship.

There, crowded on poop and forecastle, and penned in terrified droves, like cattle, between the bulwarks, swayed in passionate lamentation, the living freight, young and old—the children going to the parents, the parents to the children—the scattered members of the race flocking to their Jerusalem beyond the seas, which had for them unutterable terror, to escape from the land for which they bore such unutterable love.

"It's well for the poor devils," said Mr. Bates; "they'll be better off where they're going to. The fact is, my dear Terry, the economists have discovered there may be too much of a good thing in obeying the commands of heaven. Paddy has overdone the primæval mandate, 'Be fruitful and multiply, and replenish the earth.' The earth is not Ireland, you know."

"But I heard Major Turnbull talking at the Castle one night, and saying there was great difficulty in getting recruits; and there go, I suppose, a couple of hundred or more fine stout soldiers."

"Yes, Terry; but the supply is equal to the demand when they like to pay for it. That ship is equal to a regiment, if you let the young ones grow and count the married couples. Here we are on shore now."

The first appearance of Sweatenham College was very imposing. The long frontage of Gothic arcading, its Gothic chapel, its spires and clock-tower, the broad expanse of lawn lined with trees, the clean-swept walks, gave the establishment an aspect of importance, not to say grandeur, in my eyes, which was by no means diminished when I saw three or four of the masters strolling inside the railings in all the dignity of cap and gown, and beheld the glories of the college livery on the porter who opened the gate. It was play-hour, and from the rear of the college came the hum of voices, and the roar of the boys in the frenzy of cricket or foot-ball, pierced by the treble now and then of some youngster.

Mr. Bates came out, after a visit to the Principal which seemed to me an age, for I was expecting every moment to be summoned to his dreadful presence, and I had undergone a good deal of critical examination from several pale-faced limpid youths in trencher-caps, who were stalking about with books in their hands, and made their remarks aloud.

"I say, Grubby, he must be Irish. There's 'T. Brady, passenger, Kilmoyle to Dublin,' on that old box. Dublin is in Ireland, you know."

"I never saw such a shabby lot of traps. Did you? Perhaps his swell things are coming by next train?"

Mr. Bates's appearance delivered me from an

ordeal which I was beginning to bear very badly. He gave the driver directions to go to the Rev. Mr. Snell, Sabine Villa, and explained to me as we passed through the well ordered streets of the town of Sweatenham (which looks like a seaside town without any sea), that I was to be put in the house of the aforesaid reverend gentleman, as he had a vacancy for a boarder. "The head-master thought me fortunate in getting under Snell's roof;" and Mr. Bates added that it must be the case, for Dr. Moody spoke with such deliberation and care, there must be a meaning in every "and" or "so" he uttered.

Sabine Villa was a staring red-brick house, fenced in from the road by a wall tipped with iron spikes ; in front was a ragged space, in which gravel and grass held divided sway. At one side of the house a squat wing was thrown out, lighted by a large arched window; and a path, separated from the land by a narrow railing, led from the door of this wing to a gate opening on a lane from the main road. Ever and anon, as we were waiting for the bell to be answered, boys in trencher caps flitted backwards and forwards along the path, carrying rolls, cakes, eggs, and suspicious-looking little paper bags and baskets into the squat wing, and through the opened window came the clatter of plates and knives and forks, and a hum as of a multitude at a banquet.

A weak-eyed, feeble-legged lad, with a dirty face and a manner of great irritability, as if he were in a normal state of being aggravated, informed us that "Mrs. Snell was at 'ome, but Mr. Snell would not be back till after the young gentlemen's dinner, as he couldn't abide the smell of it," and led Mr. Bates and myself into a crypt-like parlour, filled with rigid, straight-backed chairs, a hard-looking little round table, covered with old magazines and some theological works, including "Vol. II." of "Snell's Sermons," and a small library, over which was a bust of Socrates. A portrait of a clergyman in his surplice, with a view of the sea and a Roman amphitheatre in ruins as a background, decorated one wall, and was faced by a photograph, enlarged to unusual hideousness, of a thin, flat-cheeked woman, with a small, sharp nose and round forehead, from which the hair was scooped into the fangs of a high comb presiding over the back of the head.

Mr. Bates sent up his card and a note from Dr. Moody, and after a time we were summoned to proceed to the drawing-room, where Mrs. Snell would be happy to see us.

A lady whom I recognised as the original of the portrait on the wall was seated in an arm-chair before a fire, although then it was a hot summer day. The comb had been cashiered, and the hair which had been entrusted to its guardianship, was now coaxed into three or four corkscrew curls by the side of each cheek, as if to screen the permanent blush which enriched them. Mrs. Snell wore heavy chains of gold and many rings, and gazed at us through a gold eye-glass, perched on the narrow ledge of her delicate nose, as we came in. She waved condescendingly to Mr. Bates to take a chair near at hand; but my worthy guardian, declaring he found the weather rather warm, begged to be excused going so near the fire, and Mrs. Snell was obliged to throw out a thin cold voice at him, coughing behind her hand as she spoke, and conveying an aroma of ether through the room.

" Snell is out just now; but I will give orders for Brady's reception, and that—I see his name is Brady, and that—and yours is Bates ? Well, Brady *is* Irish. We have a good many of them, and that—what illnesses has Brady had ?"

I repeated the small catalogue of my ailments, as far as I could remember them, at my guardian's request.

" That will do very nicely, and that; he's had his measles and scarlatina, and that—that's very well. His books and that Snell will look to. Mrs. Prince, my housekeeper, will attend to his clothes, and that, and his things will be all put away. I look to diet and all that as my own share. Perhaps, Brady, you had better go now and find your way to your room. Any one will tell you where Mrs. Prince is, or you may ring the bell and ask the page, and that."

Mr. Bates's face wore a quaint look as I left the room. I wandered into the hall, and having no earthly notion of Mrs. Prince's whereabouts, was about to open the parlour door to ring the bell, when the pale footman appeared in the passage, and exclaimed—

" Hullo! I say, none of that. If Snell saw you going into the parlour after you've entered, there would be a row, I can tell you. It's against the rules; and rules is rules here, I can tell you."

I had serious notions of boxing the ears of the gentleman in the olive livery and yellow waistcoat, but my purpose was checked by the entrance of a middle-aged woman, at the rustle of whose silk the footman became exceedingly exasperated.

" Mrs. Prince, ma'am, I caught this young genelman—a new boy, ma'am—goin' into the private parler——"

" That will do, James; you may go."

There was something very mild in the tone of Mrs. Prince's voice, and yet there was something very decided, and James retreated through the green-baize door with his anecdote unfinished. I had time to survey the speaker, and to see that she was a plump, middle-aged person, with a widow's cap, and an air of sleekness and composure about her, as though all went well with her. She had a kindly look too, and as I met her gaze I rejoiced that there was such a pleasant person in the Sabine Villa.

" Your things are taken up and put away in your room," she said. " They were badly packed up, and most of them will require marking. Have you had your dinner?—yes! Well, then, come, and I will show you your room. It is fortunate you have a good set with you this half. There will be Seton Sinclair, Scotch—a sturdy, fine lad; Langley, working hard for prizes; and Mowbray, doing nothing, and spending too much money, spoiling his teeth and stomach, but not doing any mischief—at least, as far as I know; and you will get on well if you make friends. 'Agree with thy enemy quickly,' you know; and all boys at school are enemies to the new-comers."

Shall I ever forget the first morning! A bell was tolling as if for the execution of a criminal: it was the first bell for prayers. The day that was about to open upon me was full of terrors; I had heard of all kinds of trials to which I was to be subjected ere the sun had set. I was "to fight Massingberd"— he was the last boy at Wickens's. It was the rule that the last boy at Snell's and the last boy at Wickens's should engage in combat if they were at all of the same size and years, and Massingberd and I answered the conditions pretty well, except that he was older and I was bigger. Then I would have to give a supper in the evening. It was against the rules of the school to do so, but it was the rule of the house for a new boy to stand treat; and I had confessed myself the possessor of five golden sovereigns, which Mr. Bates had slipped into my hands ere he drove away. There was also an intimation that I should provide a considerable entertainment at Figgis's, the pastry-cook's, which was "out of bounds;" but Talbot, junior, would run the blockade with a sovereign and carry in the supplies. I was also to shy shillings into the diving-pool, and to take a header into the Sally Hole. I was to join the cricket club—to become a member of the Junior Sweatenham Foot-ball Club—and to be tried with Burley *tertius* with a pair of sculls on the river—and I was to be examined by "Moody," to see what class I should join. All these and other matters had been confided to me at tea the previous evening, when I returned from seeing my good guardian, Mr. Bates, off on his journey home.

"Terry, my lad," quoth he, "you are big enough to take care of yourself. I need not tell you to work hard, for you have no one to look to but yourself. You will see a lot of young scamps here who do nothing; and you will see, too, I'm sure, a fair proportion of fellows who are determined to get on in the world; and you will have to decide which lot you will belong to. I have no doubt of your choice. Try and keep friends with all, but let none of them—I'm sure I need not say this—bully you or insult you. If you act like a lad of honour and spirit, you will always find plenty of lads to stand by you and prevent your being bullied. Play at their games with all your might, and when fun is over, work with all your might too, and you need not fear for the future."

CHAPTER XIII.

FULL of these sage counsels, I had returned to Sabine Villa just as the bell was ringing for tea, and met a rush of boys in the narrow lane which nearly carried me off my legs. The tide bore me into the study, as it was called—the great white-washed room inside the squat wing—in which were rows of benches and deal tables spread with cups and saucers. At one end was a raised seat and desk, at the other a kind of pulpit, and the wall was adorned with tin sconces and a large black board smeared with chalk. At the end of the centre table sat an angry-looking young man, with a red, blotchy face, straight light hair, and feeble sight, so like " Dowly," the footman, that the boys did not hesitate to assert the latter was the unacknowledged brother of Snell, taken in to economize the family arrangements. " Snell " was dressed in black, and

wore a white tie, and a college-gown, which gave him
a clerical, but not a reverend appearance; and he
glowered down the tables, which were lined by
double files of boys, face to face and back to back,
in a manner which indicated intense animosity to
his youthful charges.   Enormous cauldrons, filled
with a preparation of water and some unknown
leaf, which would have been tasteless had it not
been mawkish, were placed at the head of each
table; and mounds of coarse-looking bread, cut in
slices and smeared with a composition known to the
consumers as " Snell's compound ointment," were
erected at intervals along the line.   Dowly, as the
footman was called, assisted by a small boy, who received secret kicks, pinches, and hair pullings,
delivered by unseen legs and hands, had charge of
the arrangements, under the supervision of Mr. Snell.

" Grace !" shouted the latter, in a sharp, jerking
voice.   " Brady, grace !"

It was the rule for the last comer to say grace;
but as I knew nothing of it, and had crept quietly
into my place, " No. 39," where my mug and plate
were laid, this sudden call quite upset me.   Mr.
Dowly laid before me a dirty card, on which was
printed the formula to be used, and I was about to
commence, when my neighbour clapped his hand on

my mouth, and said—"Don't. By Jove, Snell will be down on you. You must go to the desk." With the consciousness that all eyes were upon me, and quickened by the smart tap of the master's rule on the table, I made for the desk, card in hand, and proceeded to read the grace. At first there was silence; after a word or two I was aware that there was a little tittering; then the benches seemed to shake; and at last a roar of laughter interrupted me in the midst of my task. In vain Mr. Snell thumped the table and called for silence; the merriment continued unabated; and at last I descended from my rostrum, and in obedience to the master's hand, sought my place again.

"What is it all about?" whispered I to my neighbour. "Why are you all laughing?"

"Oh! it is lovely. It's better than a play."

"What is? What is it?"

"What is it?—why, your brogue! I never heard anything like it since once I was taken to the play to see Power."

I was aware, indeed, that there was a peculiar rhythm in my way of speaking. I had been brought up in a district where the pronunciation of English was subjected to remarkable inflections; but it did not occur to me that there was anything very ludicrous in the fact.   At Dr. Ball's we did not laugh at M'Cracken, the son of the Town Major, who spoke Glasgow ; nor at Bull, the son of a clerk in the castle, whose speech was pure Somersetshire. As I ate my bread and drank my Snell's peculiar, my thoughts dwelt on the future in store for me if every word I said was to be the signal for inextinguishable laughter on the part of my companions.   The meal was over, and what was called study commenced ; but I was excused, as I had no books, and I sat watching my future companions with all the earnestness which marks a boy's investigation of his fellows.   It is well that the boy is not the father of the man.   In the little world of which I was a new citizen, there was such selfishness and trickery as would render men contemptible and hateful.   Looking at the rows of youthful faces— ugly, handsome, and neither—apparently bent over their books, one could scarcely imagine that so many of these studious youths were engaged in the most strenuous attempts to do anything but learn their lessons.   One fellow was doing his Euripides with a crib ; another had a key for his verses ; a third was getting his Horace " done " by one of the senior boys, whom he was to reward with a tip.   Of course there were some hard-working lads in the mass, striving to read as well as they could amid the secret volleys of paper pellets, and the petty persecutions to which they were subjected unseen of the Reverend Snell, who was engaged in revising the proofs of a " New Grammar," which all the boys at Sweatenham were soon to be compelled to buy at twice its cost price. How many toiling fathers, who were depriving themselves of comforts and screwing " the house" to keep their boys at college, were then solacing themselves with the thought that they would reap their reward in seeing their old age crowned by the success in life of their sons ! How many fond mothers were thinking and dreaming and praying, morning and night, for the welfare of those who were only scheming in order to make the least possible use of the advantages for which so many sacrifices had been made at home !

There was Whittley, whom his father, as he worked in his chambers, or perambulated Westminster Hall with his lean bag in hand, fondly believed to be reading hard for the college exhibition and a scholarship, engaged in the perusal of a *Racing Calendar*—a keen hand at making a book—for ever dodging to get off to the little races about Sweatenham, and conversant with the way of the turf—the humble follower of Mr. Meggs, one of the grooms in Lord

Weatherby's stable, and quite certain to be plucked for his " Little-go."

Jack Asgill, the only son of the widow of a naval captain—who was living at a little cabin by the seaside dignified by the name of a cottage—was the champion on the river, a fine, bold-spirited fellow, the leader of all the athletic sports of the college, a universal favourite, but very little calculated to wear the clergyman's gown for which his mother designed him, that he might get the benefice which a friend of his father's had promised her. Each half, the poor lady strained her eyes over the printed report of Jack's collegiate efforts.

" General Progress : M."

" What is ' M.,' John, my dear !"

" ' M. ?' Oh, ' M.' means moderate. There's ' V. G.' and ' G.' are better; but ' B.' is worse, and ' V. B.' very bad. So, you see, I'm rather high, mother."

He is rewarded with a grateful smile, and a kiss on his sunburnt cheek.

" Boarding-house Report," she goes on, " is, I see—' Unsatisfactory.' Oh, John, my love, I'm so grieved. How is that ? I'm so sorry——"

" There now, don't be a dear old goose of a

mater. That's old Snell; no one cares for that. It is all because we had a tremendous jolly supper-party the night before we came away, and some fellow threw a bolster at Snell. He thought it was me, and so down he pops me—the spiteful beast—as ' unsatisfactory.' Really, mother, that means nothing at all. Look at my place in school, and see."

"Class Master's Report," she goes on: "He might do better—moved up a division in his half."

Jack meets her inquiring glance with an easy smile. "There, isn't that first-rate? Moved up a division, mother, eh!"

"Yes; but, my boy, ' he might do better.' How is that?"

"Oh, of course, I might have moved up to the very top, if I could. You must remember, dear mother mine, that I had the deuce of a cold from that wetting I got" (the outrigger upset with him on the river) "just before the examination. And nothing pleases old Mouldy Bill—that's the name we give Venables, who has the class I'm in—he's such an awful clever chap himself. Read on, mother; it's a jolly report this time, I can tell you."

The confiding mamma continues: " Place in class of twenty-seven boys—sixteenth."

" There! sixteenth! I'm above eleven fellows.

Tibbs, who is two years older, is below me; and all the other chaps are first-rate. I was nineteenth, you remember, last half."

Mrs. Asgill sighs gently, and coughs for fear Jack would think she was at all disappointed. "Greek—B. 'B.' is bad, John, is it not?"

"That's Mouldy Bill again, mother. I hate Greek anyway; but it was a horrid chouse to give me a B., for I did my Euripides first rate."

"Latin—B.," she reads and pauses, whilst Jack breaks out, triumphantly—"Yes; but I was 'V. B.' last half; and Flack swears I've got on famously. I will be sure of 'G.,' or maybe, 'V. G.,' next half."

"Mathematics—V. B.," Mrs. Asgill gulps out, with a quaver in her tone indicative of great concern. "I always heard mathematics were highly necessary for a clergyman, and that you can't get into Cambridge without them."

"Then, darling mother, you are quite wrong. It's classics you want for the Church; anyway, I know more mathematics than old Flack, who is a clergyman; and Snell can't do a proposition in Euclid, and they say he'll get a bishopric somewhere abroad very soon. The sooner the better, say I; for our grub is beastly. I'm half-starved."

This was a masterly stroke, for it led Mrs. Asgill at once away to the question of dietary, and her face grew wan with alarm as she detected in the sinewy frame of her son evident traces of Snell's stinginess in the matter of beef and mutton.

I didn't know all this about the boys at the time, but I heard plenty of such stories after I was a few days at the college; and I saw, too, that some of the hardest-working fellows were those who had least need to provide for themselves in life.

Prayers came at last. He who knows the secrets of all hearts can judge how many knelt before Him with any thought of asking for grace and protection, or of what Snell was thinking as he jerked out in a snappish, irritable way the words of the College Litany. Then we trooped off to the dormitories, and went through the form of going to bed; but when the lights had been out in my room for half an hour, I heard the scraping of a match, and Rundle, my next neighbour, summoned me to the banquet which I had provided.

"We have it in the kitchen, so as Snell mayn't hear us. We've tipped Dowly and Cookey with two 'bob' a-piece of your tin. Put on your jacket. Follow me. Mum's the word—as light as you can." And putting his bit of candle in a tiny dark lantern which he took from his box, Rundle led me along the passage, the eye of light preceding him, and the whole transaction having that semblance of burglary which made it very agreeable to my comrade, famous as he was for his acquaintance with the deeds of "Three-fingered Jack," "Dick Turpin," and the heroes of the *Newgate Calendar*. I knew it was all wrong. I did not care for the supper; but I was too weak to resist; and many of us are led astray, not because we like to take the wrong path, but because we are not strong enough to shake off the hand which is guiding us.

It was a banquet indeed! The kitchen gas was alight, the large table covered with a cloth that had seen some service upstairs, a grand array of tin pannikins and plates, and a miscellaneous display of edibles, in which a large pie, a pile of tarts, hot sausages, and a cold fowl, were conspicuous. Bottles of ginger and currant wine were mingled with pots of marmalade and jam. The guests were all assem_ bled, mostly big boys I had seen at the upper end of the room, and took not the slightest notice of me; the kitchen door was shut carefully. Rundle surveyed the table as he took his place, and pointed to a seat on the bench.

"How is this, Winter," he asked in a low tone of displeasure, "no oysters? I wouldn't give a farthing for a supper without oysters."

"Most votes carried, Possy!" (my friend was præpositus of a class, and was generally addressed by this familiar name). "Pat's money was very little, you know; and there's such a jolly lot of cholera about: lobsters are awful cheap. Look at these five I got from Finn's for six and sixpence, cracked and cut up so as not to make a row."

Rundle was amenable to argument, and with an injunction not to make a clatter with the plates, and to talk low, the feast began. It must be admitted that a boy's enjoyment of the pleasures of the table is not dependent on agreeable society or brilliant iconversation. He eats and drinks for the sake of himself, not of his company; and silence rather enhances than diminishes his zest. And so, serious as savages, we sat and revelled in large platefuls of incongruous meats and in beakers of dreadful drinks, regardless of the morrow, and quite content with our enforced abstinence from an interchange of ideas. Everything was said in whispers. "Nubbles, I say, what a chouse you are; that's the last Banbury; you had two before." "Pass the marmalade this way, and a sweet biscuit."

If any sound above a whisper was heard, Dowly, who was thrown out as a vidette in the passage in his night-shirt, so that he might pretend he was coming to see what was the matter if Snell operated a descent on us, appeared with a pale face at the door and uplifted finger, and hissed out, " I say; now then, he's a-turnin' in bed, I can tell you. I hcerd that laughing quite plain through the door, so I did."

These interruptions and admonitions could not damp the enjoyment, which was at any rate not protracted; for in an amazingly short space of time the bottles were drained, the lobsters were but shells, the fowls but bones, the cheese but rind, the jam pots emptied. The assembly of Sybarites broke up, and one by one filtered through the doorway and glided away to their rooms, to face the horrors of nightmare or to sleep in peace, according to their digestions; and as I followed Rundle, who closed the rear, I saw Dowly ravaging among the dishes, and searching in vain for any satisfactory remnant of the feast.

Our breakfast was very like the tea of the previous night. It was a wonder to me to see the composed, innocent look of the young fellows in chapel, and above all, the guileless look of Rundle, who, as one of the choir, wore a white surplice; I knew that some of them, at all events, had been sitting up till all hours, with their heads up the chimney in their rooms, smoking, and that Rundle had gone off with a bottle of the college grocer's sherry and another of brandy under his arm, and had not retired to bed till daybreak. The array of masters in their gowns, the awful presence of Moody himself—a large sleek man, with black eyes and heavy beetling eyebrows, and a sallow face—impressed me immensely. I repented greatly of my rashness in venturing to look at him earnestly, for he suddenly caught my eye, and stared at me with an expression so severe and tremendous that I felt quite weak about the knees, and blushed till my ears tingled.

The service was over, and we marched from the chapel to the main building to the sound of a funereal bell. The head of the column passed through the arched door, and as my turn came I saw two of the boys at each side with pencil and paper engaged in ticking off the names. As I walked in one of them asked me sharply for my name.

"Oh, Brady? You are to go in to Dr. Moody at once, d'ye hear? Room A. Now then, sharp, Paddy."

The hum of voices sounded in my ears like the rushing of waters; and twice I put my hand on the door and withdrew it, for somehow or other I fancied the black-eyed, stern-faced man knew of our doings, and would visit on me all the sins of the night's dissipation. At last I was inside the dreaded portal and face to face with the doctor, who was standing at his desk looking over the exercises of the upper form, young men rather than boys, who were going up to the University. He saw but took no notice of me, and went on with his examination of the papers before him, whilst I underwent a different examination from the young gentlemen who were awaiting the results of his criticism.

What the deuce were they laughing at? I could not see anything to laugh at. They did, for neither the cut of my jacket nor my boots, nor the colour of my tie, nor my pantaloons, were familiar to these young Brummels, who had no idea of the fashions prevailing at Kilmoyle, or knew that Andy Kane, the tailor, took all his designs from the plates in "The Magazine of Taste."

Dr. Moody raised his head and beckoned me to approach.

"Your guardian tells me," he said, "you were

considered by Dr. Ball to have made fair progress. Dr. Ball is a good scholar—in fact, for one of the alumni of the Silent Sister, he may be termed an elegant and accomplished scholar; and his edition of 'Bion'—a pretty trifle—is known to us over here. What were you reading when you left ?"

I stammered through my list.

" Hum !—that sounds very fairly; quite up to our fourth form. Now, Brady, let me hear you read and translate. Begin there."

The passage in Juvenal which Dr. Moody pointed out to me was one I knew tolerably well; and, with confidence somewhat restored, I began to read aloud as I was desired. Before the second line was well begun I was aware of a titter among the Brummels, which soon became a roar of laughter, as Dr. Moody, with his hands to his ears, exclaimed—

" There, there !—that will do ! Such quantity ! Dear me, how very dreadful ! We must set at work at once on this !"

In fact, my pronunciation was of the broadest— or of the flattest Continental — type, and my prosody was feeble. I was much ashamed; and when I was called on to read a chorus from the

CHAPTER XIV.

THE FLIGHT.

"I really do not know whether we can overlook this insubordinate and quarrelsome spirit much longer," said Dr. Moody. "You are never happy except you are engaged in personal conflicts—one of those ' in bello gaudentes, prœlio ridentes.' "

"They will not let me alone, sir—they are always at me."

"At you, sir?—at you? What do you mean by that? Here have you been reported for fighting with Ricketts, Botcher, Wylie primus, the two Crawleys, within this quarter—not to speak of your boarding-house squabbles."

"There are more than those, sir. You only hear when I have the best of the fight. You don't know that I have been licked by ever so many of the big fellows, because I wont stand their making game of me."

18—2

"It is a dreadful spirit!" ejaculated the principal—"a dreadful spirit—a word and a blow. You have, I find, received corporal punishment about once a week, and have had the most severe impositions, and yet you persist in these encounters."

"If I were to be killed on the spot, or to die, sir, I cannot help it. Why are they allowed to persecute me—to ridicule, and sneer, and jibe at me? I've borne it as long as I could. Some of the fellows have left off, but others will not; and if you could only know how I am tried you would punish my tormentors, and not me."

"You say you have been fighting with the senior boys, and have been beaten—who were they?"

"I cannot tell you, sir. Some of them had black eyes as well as I had."

"Black eyes! why it's your invariable condition, sir. It is disgraceful to the college. I will promise you this: bring up before me any boy who annoys you without a cause, and I will inquire into the case and inflict on him condign punishment, if he deserves it. You may go; the last five hundred lines are condoned."

I went forth from the presence with a burning sense of wrong. In that hard time Mrs. Prince had been my only comforter.

"What! another black eye?" the good matron would exclaim, "and the yellow scarcely gone off the last one yet. That's near two pounds of raw beef I've had to pay for out of my private pocket. Why, it's no eyes you'll have at all very soon, you dreadful Brady."

The poor soul had some Hibernian tendencies herself—they stopped short of black eyes—but her encounters with Mrs. Snell, and Dobbs, the cook, and Grimes, the head chambermaid, were frequent and stormy.

It was on the evening of the day I had been in to Dr. Moody—hang these doctors, my life is weary of them!—I was working away at my desk. Dowly came in with a tray full of letters to Snell, who examined each before he called up the boy for whom it was intended. We all knew the postman's ring, and every eye was directed to the desk.

"Has Jones got his tip, I wonder?" "There's a black seal for Kimmis; his governor's been seedy." "Look at little Mac! he's got a post-office order, and a lot of stamps."

"Brady?" called out Snell. "Two letters—one from India, with a shilling to pay."

I walked up to the desk. There was a letter

with a large black seal; it was from Mr. Bates. There was another in a clear sharp handwriting, which made me start as I took it up.

I went back to my seat. I looked at the last letter again and again. With hesitating hand I tore it open, and read :—

"Auripore, June 10th, 18—.

"MY DEAR SON,—I write to you in the hope that you have not quite forgotten you have a mother. Some day when we meet I will tell you, my dear son, why I thought it best for your welfare that I should not cast any part of the burthen of my sad fate upon you; and no doubt you have been taught to hate me, and have been told I did not care for you. My dear Terence, I will not say a word against your grandfather. He was your dear papa's father, and he took a strong part against me because I made the greatest sacrifice that a woman could make for his son and for you; but I have never ceased to think of you and to love you. Though so far away, I have taken care of you as well as I could. My servant used to tell me about you; and when he was sent away I had friends who took care to let me know of your welfare. I cannot tell you how I suffered when the

news came that you were drowned; but that was
soon set to rights. I was very sorry, too, indeed,
when I heard of my father-in-law's death, though
he was not kind to me. I am told you are growing
tall and strong, and that you are very like your
father. I am glad to hear that; for I have
been unhappy about you. You are my son, and
by your father's wishes I was to take charge of
you; but I was not able then, and I only live now
to see you, and show how your poor mother loves
you. I cannot leave this country, for I have no
money, and live on the kindness of my friends;
but I trust you will be able some day to help me.
You are going into the army, and you must come
out to India; and then we will return together,
and live together always. You will be a very rich
man some day. Look after your property, and
do not believe any one who tells you there is not
a fortune belonging to your grandfather. I principally write to warn you against the Desmonds.
Your poor father told me long ago that the
Desmonds had taken all the lands of the Brady
family. I have been told that the brother of Mr.
Denis Desmond is a great man in Ireland, and that
he is your guardian, along with a low Irish attorney.
I would come over and shield you against them if I

could ; but I want you to promise your mother not to sign any paper, or to do anything about your property without letting me know first. The Desmonds feel they have got our property unjustly. They are all as cunning as serpents. I am told there is a niece of Mr. Desmond's —a Miss Butler—who is to have all the money. She lives near you, and it is said they will try to make you marry her ; and, in that case, the Desmonds would get the estates. Of course, you are too young yet, but these bad people look a long way ahead. I am dying to hear from you. I will tell why you have not heard from me before, some day. Believe me, it was for your good. When you write direct to me, ' Mrs. Brady '—you have been taught, perhaps, to think I have no right to the name—' care of Messrs. Colville and Arbuthnot, Madras.' With tears in my eyes, I sign myself,

" Your loving mother,

" MARY BRADY."

I read this long letter again and again. The prayer-bell roused me from my study of every line. Why did she write to me now ? Why had she been silent for years ? Were all these warnings against secret machinations devised to deprive me of some unknown rights? As I read "Miss Butler's" name, and the words, "they will try to make you marry her," my cheek flushed, and I felt a little fluttering of my heart.

"How little can she know the truth!" I sighed. Marry Mary Butler! Have you not been told the truth of this hapless mother of yours? See how she seeks to arouse your suspicions of your friends! Are you not unhappy and suspicious now? Remember your grandfather's last injunctions; stern and cruel as they were, it is plain they were just. No, Terence; steel your heart. The day will come when you will see her face to face. Then you can hear and judge for yourself. If she loved you so she would not leave you in your solitude and sorrow.

Prayers were over. These reflections were my prayer.

"And may Heaven have mercy on her and have pity on me!" closed them, as I rose from my knees.

We trooped off to our rooms. My mother's letter was next my heart. I had not read the other yet, but I put my end of candle on my trunk by the side of my cot, and opened it. It ran as follows :—

"Dublin, ——.

"DEAR TERENCE,—I am sorry to say that there is no cheering intelligence to give you about Lough-na-Carra. The country is in a dreadful state, and no money is to be had at all. McTurk and Skinner, who are, you may remember, attorneys for that lady in India, have oddly enough turned up as solicitors for an English mortgagee who wants his money. In fact, I fear Sweatenham College is too expensive for us, and you must make up your mind to leave at Christmas.

"The lady I speak of has been playing some of her pranks again. She is in the hands of some smart fellows, and she has served the trustees with notice that she has equitable claims in her own and her son's name on Lough-na-Carra, which she intends to substantiate; and, actually she is going, she declares, to try Sir Richard's title to Kilmoyle by a writ of ejectment. I beg of you to enter on no correspondence with her, as I hear she intends to try and use you for her purposes. Remember your grandfather's advice, and his last request that evening! I believe he was right.

"Yours ever,

"A. BATES."

"Now, then, you Paddywhack! Put out your dip, will you!" growled a great Jewish-looking fellow, named Morris, from the next bed. "Out at once, do you hear, Mr. Potato! What's the use of your reading letters from people who can't spell?"

Mrs. Prince brought in a large piece of beefsteak for Mr. Morris next morning. It was not cooked.

There were one thousand lines of the "Odyssey" for me. I made up my mind that night.

"Here's four pound nine and sixpence; it was all I could get," said Dowly. I had now ascertained his name was Pluckley, but the Greek vocative of "slavey" had become the general way of addressing him. "The watch was one pound fifteen, and the clothes were only two pounds. I couldn't get more than a quid for all the books; the rest's for my commission, you know. You can give a good supper out of it!"

Whilst the house-boys were in the playground and I was in "The Study," as it was called, engaged, as it was supposed, on my never-ending task of writing out lines, I was preparing a short letter to Mr. Bates. I told him the story of my sufferings. I was sorry to grieve him, but I could do nothing dishonourable; I could not bear to trouble my friends. It would be better to let Lough-na-Carra go altogether. He could sell off everything except the portraits, and a few things my grand-father prized. I would write to him as soon as I had made up my mind, and had got something to do. And so, bathing the letter with tears—I knew not why they fell—I sealed up my letter and put it in my pocket.

There were three fellow-victims with me, biting the ends of their pens or scribbling away, and at intervals looking up at the open windows and envy-ing the sparrows which twittered on the branches of the old elm-tree outside.

"If any one asks," said I, "say I am gone for a walk."

"By Jove, Brady, wont you catch it if your im-position's not done this time!" squeaked little Tyrwhitt *secundus.* "You're too plucky by half!"

"Well, I dare say I shall catch it, if they catch me. Good-bye."

I walked along the passage, opened the door into the garden, and in another minute was out in the lane which led to the street. There were the secret police of the college to be evaded if I got out of bounds; but I knew Sweatenham well by this time, and turning down a cross street, I struck out on the high road to London. I shied my trencher over a hedge, took my cricket-cap from under my jacket, and walked along at a fair pace towards Todley station. I knew there would be an up-train in half an hour, and I could just catch it. As I live there is " Sweet William," our itinerant confectioner, coming towards me! I owe him three shillings.

" You're out for a spree, I 'spose, Mr. Brady? Thank you, sir. No change! Well, that is handsome. I wish you'd tell Mr. Rundle I must have the half-sovereign he got of me. It's ruination to deal with some of you young gentlemen; it is, indeed. Lor' bless you! I wont say a word of seeing you. Good evening, master."

The rail was on my right. I heard far off the whistle of the engine leaving Sweatenham; and soon the rattle of the train came along with the breeze. It was a hard race. How the black speck and its cloud of steam grew on me as I ran and looked over my shoulder! Puff! puff! puff! every breath seemed to pant over me. The station is close at hand—the bell is ringing—a country cab, with a pile of luggage and an old lady and children inside, all with eager faces turned to the train, are driving up, the driver whipping the reeking horse.

" 'Ma, there's Master Brady, of Snell's."

It is one of the horrid offspring of Mrs. Mather, the wife of the college-porter.

I put on a tremendous spirt—bounded in through the door as the porter was closing it—heard a cry of despair from Mrs. Mather and the children.

" Second-class to London."

" No second-class, this train. First-class from Todley to London. Now, sir, be quick !"

The bell rang ; with another bound I was on the platform, leaped into a carriage as the guard's whistle blew and in a minute more, as I sat wiping my fore-head, the die was cast. The express-train was rattling onwards to London. My companions stared at me ; a stately old woman, whose novels I had dis-turbed—a young gentleman, her son, on whose foot I had trodden—a pretty little girl dozing in the corner. The latter just looked up ; I was certainly not the ideal of her doze, for she closed her eyes again. The stately old lady was very restless. In my inadvertent haste I had selected the seat next the door which was opposite to her also ; and so, after a minute, she said, " Alfred, would you mind asking this young gentleman to move his fect a little farther back; these carriages are so narrow."

Alfred looked at me severely. My poor feet had crept like mice under the seat, and had not crept out again ere she spoke.

" Alfred, would you see if I have not left one of my books on that seat."

I had hopped up and left the seat void and open for inspection ere the sentence was finished.

But the stately old lady, who was, I discovered, the wife not the mother of Alfred (and why he sat at the opposite corner in face of the sleeping girl was what I could not understand), resolved on war. I was very hot from my race ; the carriage was like a green-house. She called on Alfred to ask me to put up the window. Then Alfred had to move a great many cloaks and straps and cases from the net over my head, and brought his waistcoat-buttons very close to my nose. Never was there such an inde-fatigable old stateliness in adjusting herself. Her little skeleton foot was a beauty which could not be destroyed by age, and so it was in a constant state of flourish. She dropped innumerable small arti-cles upon me, and glanced at me angrily as if I were the cause of their falling.

On sped the train, oscillating at the curves and

jumping at the stations, where we caught a phantasm of faces and figures, running into a mass of eyes and coats and dresses, like the visions of a nightmare; and at each swing and roll and rock of the carriages, the lady gave a little cry and clasped her hands as if for mercy. It was intolerable. After a long run of an hour the train stopped at Dinswin. There was a row of young ladies in curls behind a counter dressed with Banbury tarts, cheesecakes, sandwiches and preserves under glasscases; busy waiters, hovering about round tables laden with quaint soups and such generous fare as suits the taste of the travelling Briton in his own land. I escaped from the stately and active old lady. Ere the bell rang I had marked a vacant seat in a carriage far away, and had esconced myself in a corner. No one disturbed me as the train moved on, for my only fellow passenger remained asleep in one of the corners opposite.

I tried to think out some plan as we whirled on, but my thoughts wandered into cloudland. I counted my money—two pounds, a crown-piece, three shillings, and a halfpenny. What was I going to do? I did not know. Had I not read of many poorer than I who had made their fortune once they were bold enough to seek it in the wide

wide world?   Was there no Brother Cheeryble who would take pity on a poor lad as he gazed earnestly on a windowful of advertisements?   Was there no fortune left for a youngster who had faith and courage, and a desire to work for life and honour?

London was before me!   There was bread to be won and honour to be gained yet.   I would not tax the kindness of my friends; I would leave Lough-na-Carra to the care of those who would see I suffered no wrong in my absence, and then from some distant land I would return with untold gold and a proud name to retrieve the fortunes of my house.   I would wander to India and seek out the repentant woman, who would cast herself into my arms and drown my reproaches in her tears.   We should all be happy!   Far away in my reverie, as the Alpine village is seen from the hill-top by the weary traveller, indistinct in the evening shadows, and yet the goal to which he is tending, there was that to which I could scarce give form and sub-stance.   Would she welcome me when I returned to lay all the rewards of my toil and long-suffering at her feet?   How can I tell with what bliss my dreams survived the ordeals through which my fancy delighted to lead me?

Here was I, a runaway from school—a fretful,

angry, disappointed boy—and yet in my reverie I was a prince in fairy-land, scattering largesse all about the world and Lough-na-Carra and Kilmoyle. Would I change with that youngster opposite whose valet came to the window when we stopped, to ask "my lord" if he needed anything; and who evidently wondered what a schoolboy in a cap and jacket, and without even a railway wrapper, could be doing with his face flattened against the glass of the carriage. I do not know if I would have exchanged my dreams for any reality short of their full fruition. Would I have accepted even the ideal I dreamed of as the full satisfaction of my hopes and the end of all my aspirations?

We flew along through the night; the screech of the steam was scaring the night-owls. There was suddenly a cry which broke through my dreams. The carriage groaned under the rigour of the brakes. My companion's head was out of the window.

"There's something wrong, I think," he said. "A smash of some kind at the end of the train."

With many groans and screams, the engine whistling all the while, the train, shaking like a living creature in mortal agony, halted at last. There was a tramp of feet, a flashing of lights—

voices crying, " Guard ! what is the matter ?—is there any danger ?"

" By Gad ! I say, there *is* a smash," repeated my lord, and leaped out at his side of the carriage. I followed him. Down in the dark the lamps were glaring, and then arose a tumult as of an agitated crowd. The citizens of the moving world had been roused by the crash as when an earthquake summons the sleepers to death. Swarming from the carriages they came forth and thronged the narrow line. Above cries of alarm and terror rose through the night air the moan of the engine, and the fierce hissing of the steam. Alas ! what a sight it was. The carriage I had left was the last but one. Turning a curve in a steep embankment, the coupling which held it and the van had broken. There was a pile of broken wood and ironwork heaped up against the bank of earth.

In the midst of all that ruin there were the dying and the dead. I stood staring vacantly at the shapeless destruction before me. Am I an evil genius ? Do I sow misery and death in my path ? I was pushed aside by strong men. When I heard the guard exclaim—" Will any one run to Langley, and give the alarm ?—straight up the line, nigh four miles away !" I was off like a deer, and outstripped my rivals in the race. I was glad to escape from the horrid scene.   I had seen the fair young girl drawn forth. Oh! let me not dwell on it. I ran through the night, fast by the road side along by the embankment, from which I could see lights in houses far away, where perhaps there was mirth, and happiness, and revel; through deep cuttings, into which the stars alone shone from above; through a dark, dripping tunnel, filled with the vapours of the night, in which my footsteps echoed along the vaulted roof. Once or twice I passed men at crossings, or seated by their fires, and startled them as I ran by, panting, with scarce voice enough to cry out— " An awful accident! Help! help! Down the line"— and so ran on. My feet tripped on beams, on bars of iron, on sleepers and heaps of ballast. I was on my legs again regardless of bleeding hands and feet. On and on, and still no town in sight—no glare of lamps—no sign of succour; but on a sudden turn there came in view an array of lights, green and red, and the gas burning cheerily along the station platform. I sped along with a fresh effort. There was no one on the platform. Crying out, " Help! help!" as I ran, I passed door after door, till a handle yielded, and I was in a blaze of ight—the first-class waiting-room, with its listless or sleepy occupants, waiting for the London train. I could scarce speak; the place appeared to whirl round me. "For Heaven's sake—Help!—Help! A dreadful accident!—Bishopshope! four miles away." I was faint and bleeding; I had eaten but little that day, and had husbanded my little store. I saw terrified eyes glaring upon me; I heard voices —a hundred questions. There was a cry, " Get him wine! Send for a surgeon!" I remember no more.

There was a stranger sitting by my bedside, when I recovered my senses. I was in a strange room, neat, and clean, and small; a dapper little maid, with her hair tucked under a white cap, held a cup in one hand, and a candle in the other, close to the bed. The stranger had his fingers on my wrist, and removed them.

"He's all right; no lesion of any consequence. I must go off to assist at once. You may give him some beef-tea or soup in an hour or so; and I will come to see how he is in the morning."

I was wide awake; one hand was bound up; I felt a bandage on my knee; but otherwise I was only conscious of a great desire to eat.

" Tell me, sir, if you please, are many people injured?"

" We fear so. Telegraph reports some fatal

cases. Thank your stars you have escaped. Good-bye for the present, and keep quiet, and get a good night's sleep."

The little maid stood still.

" What have you got there, please, Mary ?"

" Physic. My name's Anne, not Mary."

" Well, Anne, will you, if you please, throw away that physic, or keep it for the doctor. I am starving. Tell me where I am, who you are, and if I can get anything to eat, and what time it is, and all about the accident."

" Why it's only ten minutes or so since you scared the first-class waiting-room. Mrs. Pitcher, in the bar, hasn't come to herself yet. Every one in Langley's gone off to Bishopshope. The train from London arrived just after Mr. Stock, the doctor, came, and they've all gone to the place."

" But where is this ?"

" The Station Hotel, to be sure. I'm the second chambermaid. Mrs. Jolly, our first, is looking after beds, and hot water, and things, for it will be a heavy night for us. Dear me, I'm quite afeered to think when the trains do come in. All your clothes is spoiled ; but we must wait till the luggage comes for a change."

" Anne, I'm dreadfully hungry."

" The doctor said you was to have chicken-broth, or the like of that, in an hour."

" I tell you I shall die. I fainted, I suppose, from want of something to eat. Can't you, Anne?—do get me something ; and do—do at once !"

The little maid nodded her head, and laughed.

" Thank you, Anne."

In a little she came in, bearing a tray with half a cold fowl, and a small decanter of sherry, and put it on the bed. I perceived for the first time I could not use my hand. Anne saw the state of the case at once. She cut up the fowl for me, and smiled and nodded her head at every morsel I took, helped me to wine, raised her plump hands in wonder when I asked for more, and with a " Well, I never !" and a pleasant laugh of wonder, trotted off for fresh supplies, and repeated the process.

There came the slow measured puff of an engine ; the station bell rang, and was answered by all the bells in the hotel. Little Anne turned very pale.

" *They're* come," she said. " This is the third time we've had *them* here. I do dread it, to be sure. But I must go now. The waiters are back, and if you want anything in the night, one will come."

I could not rest; I got up and listened. There were heavy feet moving slip-shod, as if carrying burthens; there were cries and moans of agony; doors were shut and opened. The night was awful. How could I sleep, and think that close to me were those in mortal agony, expecting Death, the Comforter? But I crept back to my room at last, and closed my eyes.

Mr. Stock found ·me quite well, all but a cut hand and knees, in the morning. Two persons were killed—one, the girl who sat in the corner, and who was going up to meet her father, an officer returning from India; the other, an aged clergy-man, journeying to London to thank a friend for the gift of a preferment. Four passengers were so hurt that their lives were in great danger; and ten had received contusions and injuries more or less serious. There was to be a coroner's inquest; and there was to be a Government inquiry; and I was to be examined, for my activity was spoken of, and it was supposed I could depose whether the guard, and the driver, and the stokers were drunk or sober, cool or collected; whether the signalman at Bishopshope was on his post, and many particulars of the kind, as to which I had not the smallest knowledge.

Langley next day was full of mourners, of grief-stricken, anxious relatives and friends. The doctors were busy—the local men swarming in and out—the great London Lamas coming in state in special trains, and flying back again. The inquest was over. I told all I knew. When I gave my name and address, Sweatenham College, the coroner looked grave.

" You will observe, gentlemen, the witness is absent from the college, as I happen to know, for my son is there—in Term time without leave, and he is Irish. We must be cautious."

The coroner seemed to imply that I was somehow implicated in causing the accident.

I had been cross-examined at great length, till I thought some one must entertain doubts whether the poor people were killed at all. I left the room in which the ancient institution of the realm was holding its 'quest, careless of their decision, for it was little matter to me whom they found guilty. An unfamiliar voice pronounced my name. Looking round I saw a young man whom I had observed in the room busily engaged in taking notes, and who was much talked at by the coroner and by Mr. Maws, the company's solicitor, who was striving to make out that the accident was a natural result of railway travelling.

He was a good-looking, pleasant young fellow, of two or three and twenty, stoutly built, of the middle size, with curly head and light-brown whiskers, and was dressed in rather extravagant colours—a bright olive frock coat, blue cravat with diamond pin, grey trousers, and patent leather boots.

"I hope you will excuse me for the liberty, but may I ask when you are going up to town? My name is Standish—Staples Standish, and I am down here reporting the case for the *Hercules;* but I am going up by the next train, and if you'll pardon me,"—he hesitated for a moment—"we might travel together. I want to ask you a few questions, if you'll be so good. They've brought in a verdict of 'Murder' against the engine-driver, the stoker, and the guard of the train, but no one minds coroners' juries' verdicts much."

I had just been thinking what I was to do for money. There was my hotel bill; there was my ticket to be paid for; I had only to go back to Sweatenham or write to Mr. Bates.

" I really don't know when I shall leave, or which way I am going, sir."

Mr. Standish stopped.

" That's odd, isn't it ? You are very young, and of course I can't presume to offer an opinion; but it seems to me rather odd."

And so it did to me. I could not tell what I was doing, or what I intended to do. Naturalists tell us that the force which drives forth the birds of the air to cast themselves loose on the world is some sort of magnetic impulse, and that the creatures which speed over land and sea till they find rest, and fill our groves with songs of love and praise, are not conscious of their own efforts. How many fail in the way—how many, battling in vain with the storm, are swallowed up in the night-wave ? I was like one of those birds—scarcely conscious of danger, I was flying I knew not where.

" The company, of course, will pay your hotel bill and railway fare, and make your parents full compensation, if required, for any injury you may have sustained," said Mr. Maws, who had sought me out on the platform as I was walking up and down with Mr. Standish. " We may require your evidence, so you'll favour me with your London address ?"

" I have none—I know no one in London, except
it be Sir Richard Desmond; or there's Captain
Window, Royal Navy.   He lives somewhere there
too."

" Give me, if you like, in case your friends are
not in town," said Mr. Standish.   " You know
my address, Maws—1, Old-court, Temple. What
are the company going to stand for personal injuries to him, eh?   Look at his hands and knees—
cuts—contusions—loss of services—There is matter
for a parent or guardian to make money out of!"
continued Mr. Standish.   " I would not take less
than 500*l.* down if I were either of them for his
injuries."

Mr. Maws smiled, and rubbed his hands.

" You gentlemen of the press are so very full of
spirits!   In case you are needed, sir, I will write
to Sir Richard Desmond, whom I happen to know.
Good morning, sir!   Good morning, Mr. Standish.
If you could say (*sotto voce*) that you know who
attended to watch the case on behalf of the company, and with his usual tact, et cætera, et cætera
—you understand me? — I should really be
obliged. · Good evening, and safe journey."

And Mr. Maws hurried back to his coroner and
his jury.

"And so I would," continued Mr. Standish; 'just make them pay through the nose. Why shouldn't you?"

"But I didn't get cut in the accident. It was in running for help afterwards——"

"All the same. If there had been no accident there would have been no help needed; if no help had been needed you would not have been running for it! It is a clear case of constructive damages, as I would call them. No? Well, you are young and ingenuous. You wont take a lot of money when you can get it, and you are going to London to see people whose address you don't know—and you have got no luggage and no cash! It is quite a little adventure to meet you."

I turned away.

"I presume my actions are free—at least I intend them to be so."

"On my word, you wrong me if you fancy I meant to be critical or inquisitive. Pray do not think I was intrusive. I am half an Irishman myself, and when I heard your story I could not help thinking of a poor lad of your own age journeying up to London, too, some years ago, to look for friends whom he couldn't find; and I longed to be of help to you, knowing how friendless that lad was, and how much he would have given for a word of sympathy—ay, even for a look !"

He spoke earnestly, as he held out his hand, and the hard metallic ring had left his tongue.

I took his hand.

" Well," he said, " shall we go together ?   I don't want to know more than you like to tell me; but as I know ' the village,' I may be of use to you. *Andiam' ! andiam' !*"

There was just time to bid little Anne good-bye and to write a line of thanks to the surgeon, ere the train came up.

Mr. Standish, who seemed to exercise great influence, and to know every one, buttonholed an official whom he called " Tunks," which set me wondering if he was related to the driver of the Kilmoyle coach, and got a coupé for himself and me.   He produced an enormous pipe, and winking at the guard, who thought it necessary to inform him " it was against the rules," puffed out a cloud of smoke—

" Oh, yes ! so I have heard.   If you warn me now, and find me smoking at the next station, it will be forty shillings.   All right !   Two minutes behind time, guard.   We'll have another smash if you don't look sharp !"

I gave a little shudder. I thought of the poor sufferers who could not be moved in those sad little rooms. The train was moving on, and as I looked out of the window along the platform, I saw Mr. Bates running out of the Station Hotel towards the carriages. It was too late; he did not even see me.

"What do you see—the head master and all the police of Sweatenham, eh? You're safe for the present, anyway."

"No. It was actually my guardian. No doubt he has come to look after me. He has heard from Sweatenham, and perhaps he has seen my name in the accounts in the papers."

"Well, it can't be helped now. You will not be able to telegraph till we get to London, or, perhaps, not even then, as Langley may be closed. Now we will go to work; and if I ask you a question now and then you wont mind, I hope?"

He produced a lamp out of his bag, fastened it to the cloth lining of the carriage, lighted it, and, opening a little book, began to write, balancing it on his hand, as the carriage rocked to and fro at express speed.

"Yes," he remarked; "this is all new to you— new to most people till they see it. Of the thousands who will read at their breakfast tables to-morrow morning a full report of the proceedings of that coroner's jury so many miles away, not one, probably, will think how it has been produced. They fancy it comes of itself, like the leaves on the trees, I daresay.   I wont be in bed till four in the morning.   There's only one comfort I have— the editor will be up later than I !"

*   *   *   *

" London at last!   Here we are, my young friend.   It strikes me the best thing you can do is to take a shake down at my chambers.   It's late, you know.   They will scarcely like to take you in without luggage—a lad like you—at the hotel. 'Pon my word, it's the best thing you can do. Here, come along.   Porter ! a portmanteau, marked ' S,' from Langley.   Get a cab; look sharp !"

I was standing amidst a rush of people.   The train had burst like a shell and sent them forth. What could I do better?

" I thank you ; but——"

" But me no buts, as they say on the stage ; but come along."

The shops were all closed.   The long lines of the lamps kept watch and ward along the streets.

I looked out into the night, and wondered if there were any of those I saw flitting along as desolate as I felt. How little I knew! The bells were chiming for midnight.

"Do you hear? 'Turn again, runaway! Go back to Sweatenham!' Is that what they are saying? Well, you must have one day in London, at all events."

It seemed to me as if the streets and the guardian lights were filing on and on with us as we passed. My companion observed me in silence.

"Yes; you may well stare. That is a scene for a civilized Christian people—the envy of surrounding nations—to show to the world. That's the end of the Haymarket—the beginning and end of many a young gentleman about town," he said. "There is the chorus—'Murder! police!' Women screaming—men fighting—oaths and laughter. It's too early for the tide to run to its height yet."

The glare and the lights, and the tumult of voices—the straggling figures—the whirling crowd of men and women—passed away. In a few minutes more, threading a maze of monster carts, piled up with the spoils of the field, drawn up by the side of low colonnades, we passed down a narrow lane—then by a church—then under a grimy archway, and drew up at a dark grey, iron-knobbed gate. My companion got out and knocked. The gate slowly opened; and as I was wondering whether he was some great lord who was acting the part of the humble swain in Moore's ballad, he said—

"Here we are in the Temple. Come along. Bring up the portmanteau, cabby. Top floor, 1, Old Court."

It was a great quadrangle surrounded by sombre walls with many doors and windows.

"This is our quarter," he said. "We are among bigwigs, I can tell you. Look! Do you see that name over the door—'Mr. Twister'? That's Twister, Q.C. Great practice he has—ten thousand a year at least. There's Skittles, the parliamentary man. He makes as much. Next landing—up again; and here we are."

He turned the key in a battered old black door, over which was written, "Mr. Torrington Grubb, Mr. H. Smith, Mr. W. H. Smith, Mr. Tredgold, Mr. Standish."

"There's a lot, isn't there?" he asked, smiling. "But we are not all in at present. They pay the rent and keep their names up. I am the monarch of all I survey. There's no one to dispute my right but the treasurer of the Honourable Society of the Inner Temple. Now then, cabby, put down that portmanteau. I want to go on to the *Hercules* office. I'll be down in a minute. Mind your head against that doorway. Look out for the step—all right. And here we are."

I had been led through a small passage, and found myself in a large, low-roofed room, surrounded with book-shelves and old prints. A round table, covered with papers, and letters, and books, stood in the centre; and three easy chairs, an old sofa, and a reading-desk, completed the furniture. Over the chimney-piece was a very sombre looking-glass, stuck full of old cards, bills, and letters. The chimney-piece was garnished with pipes of clay and meerschaum; above it were sets of foils, masks, and boxing-gloves.

Standish opened a door and let me get a glimpse of a tiny bed-room, from which he emerged with a pile of blankets and a pillow.

"Now," he said, as he arranged them on the sofa, "I install you in full possession, to have and to hold as long as you like—your bed is ready inside. You will find everything that luxury can suggest or wealth procure in that cupboard: you can take the goods the gods provide you, aided by the goddess of Plenty, Mrs. Chandler. This is the key of the wine, which is the only thing I dare not trust to my deity, for if I did she would leave me poor indeed. There are more books than you can read to-night; There is a boot-jack. If you hear a noise in the morning don't mind it; I shall be coming in at all hours. We will get a fellow to look at your cuts in the morning. Sleep well—good night."

And with a cheerful laugh he closed the door; I heard his light step bounding down-stairs past Twister, Q.C., and then all was silent.

It was to little purpose I sat and thought, for my mind wandered away to the past, and then dwelt on the impossible project, which I scarcely could shape to my own mind. In that profound solitude I could not believe I was in London. I went to the window; there was a faint streak of light in the sky; spires innumerable; a forest of steeples and chimney-pots; a great dome rising to the sky, on the summit of which a ball and cross were warming into colour; a grey, cold stream, on which black barges floated away past the angle of the walls which bounded my view. These grew out of a shadowy background, and that was all.

It might be a dream of a city of the old and bygone world, in some occult desert.   Hark! there is a sound at last.   It is a song—a very husky sort of vocalization, joyous withal.   It echoes through the court below, and as it comes nearer, " We wont go home till morning ! we wont go home till morning !" Well, go home now.   It is morning already.   The sparrows twitter in the eaves and in the trees which uplift their leafy honours round the walls of brick: their day's work is before them.   The growing light as it strengthens struggles with the smoky arms raised from their chimney cradles to smother it.   As I lay down on the stranger's bed I felt I had consigned him to the ancient sofa; and thanking heaven for its mercies, I felt thankful too that in this waste so full of life I was not quite cut off from human sympathy.

END OF VOL. I.